Seven Long Years
Until College

Other Books by Mary Jane Auch

Seven Long Years Until College

Until College

Mary Jane Auch

HOLIDAY HOUSE / NEW YORK

Library of Congress Cataloging-in-Publication Data
Auch, Mary Jane.
Seven long years until college / by Mary Jane Auch.
p.   cm.
Summary: When her new stepfather imposes restrictions on her daily
life, and her best friend prepares to move to Cleveland, Natalie
takes drastic steps to stem the tide of change in her life.
ISBN 0-8234-0901-5
[1. Stepfathers—Fiction.   2. Friendship—Fiction.]   I. Title.
PZ7.A898Se   1991   91-2094   CIP   AC

For Kat, Dan, and Sunshine

Seven Long Years
Until College

Chapter One

"Natalie," Mom yelled from her bedroom. "Will you please answer the door? It must be the caterers."

"Okay, Mom." It seemed funny to barrel down the stairs without dodging the junk Mom usually had piled on the steps. It took a wedding to make Mom clean house.

There were two women in pink uniforms waiting outside the door. The fat one with "Rosie" embroidered on her pocket seemed to be in charge. "Is this the Willderby residence?" she asked.

"No, it's the Hansons'," I said.

Rosie looked at her clipboard. "Isn't this 7355 High Ridge Trail?"

That's when I realized my mistake. "This is the Willderbys'. I mean it will be after Mom gets married at eleven. Except I'll still be a Hanson, so I guess it's the Hanson Willderby residence."

Rosie set a grocery bag down on the counter. "Oh? Is your mother hyphenating?"

"No," I said. "She's upstairs shaving her legs."

The two women laughed. "I meant her name," Rosie said. "Is she going to be Mrs. Hanson-Willderby?"

"I know what you meant," I said. "That was a joke." It wasn't but I didn't want to admit it. I don't like being laughed at, especially by strangers. I grabbed a bowl and some Cheerios and took the milk from the refrigerator.

Rosie's sidekick peeked in the fridge before I got the door closed. "You don't want to put anything in here. It's packed to the brim, and I think something died on the bottom shelf."

Rosie came over and sniffed. "You're right. The butter would pick up the taste of whatever that is in the first two minutes. We'll leave everything in the ice chest. We'll be serving right at noon anyway." She turned to me. "Where does your mother keep her pots and pans?"

I sat down at the table. "I don't know. I think they're in the oven. We don't use them that much."

Rosie opened the oven door and a couple of old frying pans clattered out onto the floor. "I can see that." She rummaged through the stuff in the oven. "Doesn't your mother have a double boiler?"

"When she wants to boil water for coffee, she does it in the microwave. I guess you could boil two cups at a time, if you want to do it double." I shoved my cereal bowl to the corner of the table to make room for the stuff the other woman kept bringing into the house.

"I'm not boiling anything," Rosie said, trying to fit the pans back into the oven. "I need the double boiler to make the hollandaise sauce. I guess I can make do with this." She put water into one pan and put another pan on top of it. It looked pretty strange to me, but since Mom didn't cook much, I figured there were probably a lot of things I didn't know.

"I can't get any of these burners to work," Rosie said. "Is there something wrong with your stove?"

I finished the last of my cereal and dumped my dish in the sink. "You'll have to ask my mom. I'll go get her." I called to Mom from the bottom of the stairs.

She came down wrapped in her big terry cloth bathrobe and wearing her pink bunny slippers. With her hair wet and without any makeup on, she looked like a kid about my age. "Is there a problem?"

Rosie made a sweeping gesture. "Everything's a problem. You don't have any decent cookware, and the stove doesn't work."

"Oh, I forgot to tell you. The stove hasn't worked for some time. I keep meaning to get it fixed, but . . ."

Rosie set the pot down on the stove—hard. "How am I supposed to prepare an eggs benedict brunch for thirty people with no stove?"

Mom smiled and shrugged. "Can't you use the microwave? I cook everything that way."

Rosie's face was getting red. "If I'd known about this

ahead of time, I could have prepared it at home and brought it when you were ready to serve. It's too late for that now. We have an anniversary luncheon to do right after this. I'm already running behind."

"Never mind," Mom said. "We'll just order takeout from someplace."

Rosie started gathering up her things. "You're going to lose your deposit, and I'm still charging you for the food."

"It doesn't matter," Mom said, opening the door. "Just leave quickly, please. I don't want anything to spoil my wedding day." She pulled out the phone book as Rosie and her helper took the last of their things. "Natalie, be a dear and call McDonald's for me, will you?"

"McDonald's?"

"Yes. See if you can get them to pack up thirty of those egg and muffin things. They're sort of like eggs benedict anyway. If they won't deliver, we'll send someone over to pick them up at noon."

"Can I get a Big Mac and fries instead?"

Mom hugged me. "You can get whatever you want. I just want this day to be perfect."

Mom dashed back upstairs while I called the restaurant. I ordered extra fries and a milkshake for myself, then ordered the same thing for my sister, Christa. She hated eggs, anyway. McDonald's wasn't going to take the order until I told them my mom was getting married. Then I had to get her on the phone before they'd believe it wasn't just some sort of kid's prank. Mom even persuaded them to deliver.

When I went back upstairs, Christa was already in her bridesmaid's dress. It was pink with big puffed sleeves and a ruffle around the scooped neck, just like mine. "Aren't you ready yet, Nat?"

I went in and sat down on her bed between the open suitcase and some half-packed cartons. "The wedding's almost an hour from now. I don't want to wear that dress any longer than I have to. It itches."

Christa pulled some sweaters out of the drawer and stuffed them into the suitcase. "I can't believe I have to be in a wedding this morning and leave tomorrow morning for college. I don't know why Mom couldn't have set the wedding for sometime this fall. Most people take months to plan a wedding. She did it in a week."

"When has Mom ever planned ahead?" I said. "Besides, she wanted to have the wedding before you left. You probably won't get home before Thanksgiving." I refolded the top sweater and smoothed it out in the suitcase. "I wish you didn't have to go. I'm going to miss you."

Christa smiled. "I know. It's kind of scary. At least you'll be home with Mom and Frank where it's famil-iar. I don't know anybody at Corinthia." She pulled my hair back. "Come sit by the mirror. I'll put your hair in a french braid like mine."

I sat on the stool in front of Christa's vanity and

watched her in the mirror as she brushed my hair. She looked so old all of a sudden, and so pretty. I wondered if I'd ever look like that. We had the same hair and eyes, but they didn't look as good on me as they did on Christa. "You're the lucky one," I said. "It's going to be weird having Frank move in with us."

Christa put down the brush and started weaving my hair into a braid. "Frank's okay. He makes Mom happy."

"But he's not as much fun as Dad."

Christa poked some pins into my hair to hold the loose strands. "I think Mom's looking for security rather than fun. Dad's great, but you can never really count on him to be there when you need him. You know how he's always going off on business trips. Here, turn around." She waved a lipstick in front of my face.

"Lipstick?" I pulled away. "I'm not going to wear that stuff."

"Don't be a pain. It won't hurt to put on a little makeup for your mother's wedding." She put some blusher on my cheeks, and brushed on some eye shadow. When I turned around and looked in the mirror, somebody else looked back. It wasn't me exactly, but she was pretty.

"That's a beautiful picture." Mom was standing in the doorway, watching us. She was in her wedding dress—pale pink lace with some rosebuds in her hair. "The jeans are a bit informal, though, Nat."

"I'm going go get dressed at the last minute, Mom."

"This *is* the last minute, honey. I can hear the guests arriving, and Frank's car is in the driveway. Miss Perkins is starting to play."

Miss Perkins was my old piano teacher. As I went down the hall, I could hear the sour notes on our piano. Miss Perkins was probably having a fit about that. I could also hear Mrs. Baldwin, our neighbor, greeting the wedding guests.

I slipped out of my jeans and opened the package of panty hose Mom had left on my bed. The stockings were all shriveled up, as if they were made for a gnome woman. I sat down and slipped my right foot into one of the legs. It kept stretching, so my foot wasn't making much progress toward the toe. I grabbed hunks of material, trying to pull it up. Finally, I gave up on that foot and started working on the other one. The left leg felt funny as I pulled it up, and I saw that the panty hose had wound around my leg a couple of times. It made me feel as if I had my left foot on backward. These things should have been labeled "front" and "back." With socks, you can see where your heel and toes should go, but the feet of these things were little wrinkled blobs. I still had about six inches of panty hose dangling off the end of each foot. At least my shoes were a little big and had pointy toes, so I figured

I could stuff the extra in there. I couldn't imagine how Mom could wear these things every day to work. When I grew up, I was going to get a job where I could work in bare feet or sneakers.

I took off my T-shirt and slipped the bridesmaid's dress over my head. I thought I was going to suffocate in all the material as I groped for the armholes. The itchy ruffles made me shiver as they slid over my bare arms. This was going to be a long day!

I was struggling with the back zipper when Mom appeared at the door. "Oh, Natalie, you look lovely. I wish I could convince you to dress up like this more often."

"Right, Mom. I'm going to make a real fashion statement and wear this on the first day of school."

Mom pulled the zipper up the rest of the way and turned me around to face her. "You just don't realize how beautiful you've become. I can't believe both my girls are growing up so fast. Christa's off and leaving us, and before I know it, you'll be heading for college, too."

"Mom, I'm only going into sixth grade. I have seven more years at home."

Mrs. Baldwin called up from the stair landing. "Frank wants to know when the minister is coming. What should I tell him?"

Mom's face turned white. "Oh dear! I never told Reverend Willis."

"Mom," I said. "How could you forget the minister?"

Mom nervously brushed the hair back out of her eyes. "Well, it's just that I had all these things on my mind, with the caterer, and the flowers, and getting your sister off to college. Look, it's no problem. Don't worry about it. I'll call Reverend Willis now. He'll come. I'll tell him it's an emergency."

"An emergency is when someone dies," I mumbled, but Mom had already started dialing.

"It's an answering machine," she said, slamming down the phone. "Can you believe it? Ministers are supposed to be there when you need them."

"Maybe you'll have to call off the wedding," I said. That was wishful thinking. I knew Mom was going to marry Frank no matter what, but Frank was nothing like Dad. Dad could always make me laugh even in my worst moods. Frank sort of put me in a bad mood. He was nice enough, but just . . . well, kind of boring. I wanted Dad to come to the wedding to liven things up, but Mom said you don't invite your ex-husband to your second wedding. Except for a few neighbors and family friends, we didn't know many of the wedding guests. Most of them were Frank's friends—"business associates" he called them, people he had to invite. Mom had to take a lot of people off her list to keep the wedding small enough to have at home. Even Grandma and my best friend, Carla Ackerman, and her parents were cut from the list.

"Judge Walsh!" Mom said suddenly, ignoring my remark about canceling the wedding. "He could marry us. Natalie, he lives in that white house with the pillars, down on the corner of Benson and Elm. Run down there and ask him to come."

"Why me?" I asked. "Can't you call him?"

"I don't know the man, Natalie. He'll think I'm nuts. You can convince him. It'll be much better if you deal with him in person."

"Oh, sure. He's not going to think *I'm* nuts? Running down the street in a prom dress on a Saturday morning?"

Mom could probably persuade me to jump off a bridge if she wanted to, which, luckily, she never has. Before I knew it, I was walking the block and a half to Judge Walsh's house. My shoes felt four sizes too small as my toes pushed against the wadded-up panty hose. The pink taffeta was sticking to my skin in the last-day-of-August morning heat. I could feel strands of hair pulling out of my french braid, and the crotch of my panty hose was creeping down to my knees. This was not my idea of the perfect wedding day!

Chapter Two

When I got to Judge Walsh's house, there was a fat, bald man out in the driveway, washing a car. I'd never seen the judge before, but I didn't think that was him. I figured a judge had someone else wash his cars for him, probably a chauffeur. I started up the driveway, but before I could duck out of the way, a stream of water shot out at me from the other side of the car.

"Hey! Watch what you're doing," I yelled.

The bald head peeked over the car. "Sorry, I didn't see you. Here, use this." He tossed me a towel. "It's clean. I haven't used it on the car yet."

I tried to blot the water from my dress, but there was a big wet spot down the front of the skirt. "Mom's going to kill me," I said. "This is never going to dry in time for the wedding." My hair was dripping, making even more of a mess. I caught the drips with the towel and handed it back to him.

He used it to wipe the sweat from his forehead. "I'm

13

really sorry. I didn't even know anyone was there. Were you looking for someone?"

"I need to see Judge Walsh," I said.

"Well, you're looking at him."

"You're the judge?" Now I was sorry I'd yelled at him.

He smiled. "We don't always wear the black robes. What did you need me for?"

"A wedding," I said.

Judge Walsh looked at me and scratched his head. "You look pretty young to me. You'd need to have your parents' consent. Maybe we could get together to talk over this wedding idea."

"It's not me," I said. "My mother's the one who's getting married." I told him about how she'd forgotten to call the minister.

"I guess you are in a bit of a pickle," he said. "I certainly can't refuse you after I got your dress all wet and everything. If you wait here for a few minutes, I'll run inside and change."

"We don't have a whole lot of time," I said, glancing at my watch. "The wedding was supposed to start about ten minutes ago, and all the guests are waiting at our house."

"Then I'll just grab my robe. Won't take but a second. We can drive to your house in my car."

We had to park a little way down the street, which was a good thing because Judge Walsh jumped out of the car in his bermuda shorts. When he put on the black robe, he looked more like a judge.

Frank met us at the door. "What's going on? I couldn't ask your mother because it's bad luck to see the bride before the wedding."

"Everything's fine," I said. "This is Judge Walsh. He's going to marry you."

Frank shook Judge Walsh's hand. "A judge? I thought it was going to be Reverend Willis."

"There was a last-minute change," I said. "No problem. Don't worry about it." I was beginning to sound a lot like my mother.

As we went in the front door, Miss Perkins was playing "I Love You Truly."

"That's about the fourteenth time we've heard that song," Frank muttered. "For a piano teacher, that woman certainly has a limited repertoire of wedding songs."

Mom was waiting for me at the top of the stairs. "Did you get the judge? Is he going to perform the ceremony?"

"Everything's all set," I said.

Christa came out of her room, adjusting an earring. "Nat, what happened to your dress? It's soaking."

"I had a little run-in with a garden hose. It'll dry out."

"But not in time for the wedding," Mom said. "We're ready to start."

"This will cover it up." Christa handed me my bouquet. "If you hold it down low, nobody will see the spot." She poked the stray strands of hair back into my french braid. "There, you look beautiful."

Mom smiled. "Come on, let's get going. The natives are getting restless down there." She signaled to Mrs. Baldwin, who signaled to Miss Perkins, who started playing the wedding march. "You go first, Natalie. Don't forget to smile."

As I started down the stairs, all of the guests in the living room stood up and watched every step I took. This was worse than being up to bat with the bases loaded. My shoes had thin little heels, and they felt wobbly.

I had to hang my arms down and hunch over to make my flowers cover the big spot on my skirt. I felt like a girl chimpanzee on the way to her prom.

Mrs. Willderby, Frank's mother, was in the front row. Her gray hair was tinted almost blue, and she was built like a hen—big on the top, with little spindly legs. She took one look at me and straightened her shoulders, holding an imaginary bouquet at waist level. When I didn't take the hint, she pulled her shoulders back so hard you could almost hear her shoulder blades crunch together. If there was one thing Mrs. Willderby hated, it was bad posture. Frank always looked as if he had a steel rod shoved under the back of his suit jacket.

Frank and Judge Walsh were standing at the end of the living room by the fireplace. There were bouquets of pink carnations on the mantel behind them. I was supposed to walk in time to the music, but I just concentrated on getting to the front of the room without falling over. I guess I went too fast. By the time I got to my place, Christa was still on the stairs. Then Mom came next. Her face was pink with excitement and one of the rosebuds was slipping out of her hair, but she looked beautiful.

While I was waiting for Christa and Mom to catch up to me, I noticed Judge Walsh's shoes. He was wearing sneakers with red socks, and about three inches of his hairy legs were showing below the robe. I wasn't the only one who noticed. Frank was looking down at Judge Walsh's feet, and he didn't look too happy. Neither did Mrs. Willderby.

Christa took her place next to me, and Mom stopped beside Frank. Judge Walsh was just about to start speaking when Mom smiled and raised her hand. She hugged Christa, then came over to me. "Natalie," she whispered as she hugged me. "I forgot about the delivery from McDonald's. We're running late, so the food should arrive sometime during the ceremony. From where you're standing, you'll be able to see when somebody comes to the back door. After things get started, see if you can slip out. There's money in the blue cookie jar."

"Mom," I whispered back. "I can't sneak out in the middle of the wedding."

"Just keep edging over little by little. That way nobody will notice. And be a dear and put the food out on the dining room table, will you? It'll be fine, honey. Don't worry about it." She winked at me and moved back into place.

That was Mom's answer to everything—"Don't worry about it." Frank, on the other other hand, worried about everything. He worried about whether it was going to rain, or maybe it wouldn't rain and his grass would get brown. He was really worried about Mom putting together a wedding at the last minute. He thought they should wait and "do it right." He only gave in because Mom convinced him that it would be harder to have the wedding at Thanksgiving when everybody was tied up with their own family dinners.

I guess it's true what they say about opposites attracting. If I had Mrs. Willderby for a mother, I'd probably worry too. Frank had never been married, so he and his mother lived in the same house where Frank grew up. Mrs. Willderby always looked as if she was mad about something, and she didn't look too pleased right now. I had the feeling that it wasn't just my posture that was upsetting her.

Judge Walsh was starting a speech about how great marriage is when I heard a knock at the back door. I didn't have time to edge out quietly, so I just left.

Everybody probably thought I had to go throw up or something. That wasn't too far from the truth.

The kid at the door had two big cartons. "It's fifty-seven fifty," he said.

"Dollars?" I gasped.

"No, Japanese yen. If you can't pay, this goes back. The manager still isn't convinced this wasn't a hoax."

"No, honest," I whispered. "It's my mom's wedding. There's money in this jar." I reached inside. "Two twenties and a ten. Wait a minute. I'll have to find more."

"I'm not going anywhere until I get the money. *All* of the money," he said. "We usually don't deliver, you know. We're just doing you a favor. A *big* favor."

"Just a minute. My mom's purse is upstairs." He started to follow me into the front hall, but I stopped him. "There's a wedding going on in there," I whispered. "They'll see you."

I hadn't counted on the fact that they'd see me too. I slipped quickly up the first few steps, then skipped the next one because I knew it creaked. Only I counted wrong. Instead, I hit the creaky step full force, right at the quietest part of the ceremony. When I turned around, everybody was staring at me. So much for going unnoticed. The guests seemed to be waiting for me to do something, so I did. I threw my bouquet. It wasn't something I thought about. It just happened naturally, probably because I've watched so many old movies that show the bride standing on the stairs, tossing her bouquet.

The crowd gasped as my flowers arched through the air. Then Miss Perkins leaped up from the piano and tackled the bouquet just before it hit the floor. Everyone looked stunned for a minute, until Mom laughed and started clapping. Then everybody else started clapping as if this were something we had planned to do all along.

Miss Perkins's face was bright red as she climbed back on the piano bench, but she was smiling. The person who catches the bride's bouquet is supposed to be the next one to get married. I wasn't sure it counted if you caught the bridesmaid's bouquet, but Miss Perkins seemed to think it did. She launched into a few bars of "Happy Days Are Here Again" until Judge Walsh caught her eye. Then she folded her hands in her lap while he went on with his speech. I figured it was better to just keep moving up the stairs. After all, this wedding wasn't exactly going like clockwork.

I found Mom's purse in a jumble of clothes on her bed, slipped the money I needed out of the wallet and ran down and paid the delivery boy. I gave him extra for a tip, but from the look on his face, it wasn't enough. I never could figure out things like tips.

I peeked into the dining room. Mom had the table set with our good china and crystal and the big silver coffee urn she'd borrowed from Mrs. Baldwin. There

was another bouquet of carnations in the center of the
table. At least Mom had remembered to call the flo-
rist. I was going to unwrap all of the little muffin things
and put them on a platter, but decided they'd stay
hotter if I didn't. I piled them neatly into two big
pyramids, one on each side of the table. I left Christa's
and my burgers, fries, and shakes out in the kitchen.
I didn't want to spoil the design. I slipped back into
my spot just in time to hear Judge Walsh say, "I now
pronounce you man and wife."

Miss Perkins started in on the piano, and Frank
kissed Mom. That seemed weird. I'd never seen them
kiss before.

I followed Christa back down the aisle between the
rows of folding chairs. Then we all met out in the front
hall and hugged. Pretty soon the guests started filing
through. Mrs. Willderby was one of the first. "Interesting ceremony." She gave my mother one of those
kisses that lands in midair, and looked over Mom's
shoulder into the dining room.

That was about the same time Frank noticed the
table. "McDonald's?" he said. "I thought we were having a caterer."

Mom straightened his tie. "It was a last-minute
change. It'll be fine. It's almost the same as eggs benedict. Help yourselves, everybody."

The guests lined up at the dining room table to pick
up their little packages. Mrs. Willderby put a cup

under the spout of the silver coffee server. "This doesn't seem to be working," she said.

Mom ran her fingers through her hair, knocking out the last rosebud. "Oh dear. Coffee! I forgot about that. Christa and Natalie can make some in the microwave."

"One cup at a time?" I asked. "Mom, we'll still be serving at midnight."

"It may take a while," Mom said, waving me toward the kitchen, "but you'll manage."

Mrs. Willderby raised her eyebrows. "*Instant* coffee?"

Mom shrugged. "I'm afraid that's all we have."

Mrs. Willderby set her cup back on the table. "Never mind. If I can't have a cup of real coffee, I'd rather go without."

Mom looked at Frank. "I'm sorry. There were so many arrangements to make at the last minute . . . but let's not let it spoil our day. We'll just get into the spirit of things. After all, it's our wedding day."

When I looked at Frank's face, I could tell he wasn't exactly getting into the spirit of things. "Oh great," he mumbled. "Here comes Mr. Aldrich."

"Your boss?" Mom whispered. "The bank president?"

"That's him. When he sees we're serving fast food for the reception, he'll probably demote me to a teller."

Mom slipped her arm through Frank's. "Nonsense.

How we celebrate our wedding is our own business."

Mr. Aldrich looked into the dining room and broke into a grin. Then he slapped Frank on the back. "Willderby, I have to hand it to you. This is the most unusual wedding I've been to in a long time. It's nice to have food you can recognize at a reception, too. Some of that stuff they serve on little toothpicks is a mystery to me. I like to know what I'm eating."

Frank was speechless, but Mom spoke up. "Frank wanted our wedding to be different. Weddings should be fun, don't you think, Mr. Aldrich?"

Mr. Aldrich opened his muffin. "By all means. Glad to see you're a man with unusual ideas, Willderby. I like that. I like that a lot."

Mom just smiled.

Chapter Three

As soon as most of the guests had cleared out, I flew upstairs to change. I could take just so much of playing dress-up. I slipped out the back door and ran most of the two blocks to Carla's house.

"Up here, Nat," she yelled from the treehouse as I started up her driveway.

Carla's treehouse was the perfect kid's hideout. Of course, we weren't usually hiding out there because everybody could guess where to find us. You could see the whole neighborhood from there. I climbed the wooden ladder rungs that were nailed to the tree trunk and pulled myself up into the house.

"What are you doing?" I asked. "You could die of the fumes in here. Haven't you ever heard of air pollution?"

Carla was sitting cross-legged on the floor and had eight opened bottles of nail polish next to her. "I'm making rainbow nails." She held out her left hand with

24

a different color on each nail. "I thought I liked the maroon in the bottle, but it dries a different color. What do you think?"

"I don't know. The pink looks the most natural."

Carla rolled her eyes. "I'm not going for natural here."

She screwed the tops back on all the little bottles. "So how was the wedding?" Her eyes narrowed. I could tell she was still mad about her family being cut off the guest list.

I shrugged. "It was okay I guess."

Carla waved her fingers in the air to dry the polish. "I think it was rotten that we didn't get to go."

"Me too," I said. "I didn't know half the guests. They were mostly people Frank works with at the bank."

"Why would you invite them to your wedding instead of your friends?"

"Don't ask me! I don't have any say in what's going on lately."

Carla opened one of her bottles of nail polish. "I know how that feels. Want to do rainbow nails? We can set a new trend when school starts."

"Right. I'm sure everybody will be dying to follow our lead."

Carla finished a bright blue nail and started on a green one. "You never know," she said. "I think rainbow nails are kind of new and different." She blew on the green nail to dry it. "That's how you get accepted by an in group. I read it in *Seventeen*. They even show rainbow nails. Check it out. The magazine is in the treasure box."

I wasn't sure I wanted to be a part of the "Innies." That's what we called Berna Jean Farber and her friends Mavis, Kimberly, and Adrian—the most popular girls in the class.

Carla and I were in a group by ourselves. We had both moved to town two years ago, right after Mom and Dad were divorced and Mom got the job at the gallery. Carla and I became instant best friends. At first, we did everything we could to get noticed by the Innies, but we never got invited to join them. The other kids didn't want to join us either, so it became just the two of us. When nobody else was around, we called ourselves the "Outies." It wasn't so bad being in the out group, as long as Carla was in it with me.

I dug through the wooden crate we called our treasure box and found the magazine. "This is from two years ago. If rainbow nails were such a great idea, why didn't anybody try them?"

"Rochester is two years behind New York City," Carla said. "Besides, that makes it seem like our own, original idea. We need more colors, though. The reds and pinks look too much alike."

"I think Christa has some purple," I said. "She used to wear purple lipstick and polish, remember?"

Carla smiled. "Oh, yeah. That's when she wore all purple clothes and we called her Lady Lilac. Purple nail polish would be perfect. You think she still has it?"

"Probably. I don't think she's taking it to college with her. She's gone through her lilac period. Let's go look."

Carla closed up her bottles. We climbed down the ladder and ran all the way to my house.

The guests were all gone. Mom had changed back into jeans and a sweat shirt and was having coffee with Frank at the kitchen table. "You disappeared without a word, Natalie," Frank said. "Your mother and I were worried about you."

Mom took her cup to the sink. "Oh, Frank. I told you she'd be at Carla's. These two are inseparable. There are some leftover egg things on the dining room table, if you're hungry, kids. There's wedding cake, too."

"Your mother doesn't look like a bride," Carla whispered as we went into the dining room. Then she saw the table. "That's wild! You had McDonald's for the reception?" She opened one of the packages and took a bite. "These aren't bad cold. I'm surprised your mom had a regular wedding cake, though. It seems so conventional."

"I know." I sliced a piece of cake for myself. "She got it for Frank. He likes things to be normal."

Carla rolled her eyes. "Lots of luck finding anything normal around here. Aren't they going on a honeymoon?"

"Not really." I licked frosting from my fingers. "We're taking Christa to college tomorrow. Then we're coming right back because of school starting Tuesday. Come on, let's go find Christa's nail polish." We went through the kitchen to the back stairs.

"What are you girls up to now?" Mom asked.

"We just came home to get Christa's old purple nail polish, Mom. Is she here?"

"She's making the rounds of a few friends—saying good-bye. I doubt she'll need the purple polish anymore. She overdosed on that color a couple of years ago. What are you going to do with it?"

"We're painting on rainbow nails for the first day of school." Carla held up her blue, green, and pink-nailed hand. "We're starting a trend. I read about it in *Seventeen*."

Mom laughed. "That should make an impression. I used to have some bright orange polish. It's probably in the medicine cabinet in the bathroom."

"I may have thrown it out," Frank said. "I cleaned out the medicine cabinet the other day when I moved some of my things over here."

"You trashed our stuff without even asking?" I glared at him.

Mom patted my shoulder. "It's probably still in the

garbage. I think I'd better look through it, too. One man's trash is another man's treasure."

Frank cleared his throat nervously. "You're right. I should have asked first." He started to say something else, then changed his mind and left the room.

"Boy, is he weird," Carla muttered.

"He has no business messing with our stuff, Mom," I said.

Mom brushed the hair out of her eyes. "Just let it go, Natalie. I'm sure Frank thought he was doing us a favor by cleaning out the cabinet. After all, it was so full you couldn't open the door without something falling into the sink. We'll work things out. Meanwhile, I'm going to rescue our treasures from the garbage."

Carla and I ran upstairs and found Christa's purple nail polish on her dresser, then went back outside. Mom was loosening the tie on a black plastic bag. She made a face and pulled it tight again. "Yuck! If it's in here, it's lost forever. Frank must have cleaned out the refrigerator, too." She hauled out another bag, peeked inside and pulled out a green bottle. "What a waste. I could get at least three more shampoos out of this."

I reached over her shoulder. "I don't believe it. He threw out a perfectly good half-pack of bubble gum."

By the time we found the orange nail polish, Mom and I had rescued a whole pile of other stuff. Even Carla found some things she could use.

"If I were you, Mom," I said, "I'd be really mad at Frank for trashing all this good stuff."

Mom shrugged. "I said we'll work it out, Natalie. Marriage is give and take."

It looked to me as if marriage to Frank was going to be throw out and retrieve.

Chapter Four

"How much farther is it?" I asked, trying to shift into a more comfortable position in the backseat. Christa and I had cartons under our feet and piles of bedding stuffed between us.

"It won't be long now," Mom said. "You should be able to see the towers any minute."

"What towers?" I asked.

"They're the best dorms on campus," Christa said. "I saw them when I went for orientation last month."

"Is that where your room is?" I asked.

Christa nodded. "It's on the tenth floor. You should see the view of the lake. It's absolutely gorgeous."

"Do you know your roommate's name?" Mom asked.

"The room assignment letter said Bethany Cook. She's from Maine." Christa was fidgeting with the strap of her purse. I could tell she was getting nervous about going away, even though she wouldn't admit it.

The road wound along the shore of the lake. Pretty soon we drove over a rise. "There it is," Frank said.

The Corinthia campus was straight ahead. It looked like a castle, set way up on the hill like that. No wonder Christa picked this school. She had posters of castles hanging all over her wall at home. She always said she'd live in a castle someday. This was the next best thing.

We drove through the town and up a steep road. The towers disappeared for a while until we were almost at the top of the hill. Then we saw the big stone marker at the entrance with Corinthia College engraved on it. Christa reached over and squeezed my hand. "Can you believe it, Nat? I'm really here."

We passed a big pool with fountains shooting up from it. "Wow," I breathed. "Do they let you swim in there?"

Christa laughed. "No, it's just for show. I've heard they turn the fountains off after Parents Weekend in November."

The engine of Frank's car groaned under the strain of our load on the steep grade. "I wouldn't want to be driving this in winter," he said. "Only a mountain goat could make it to the top."

Christa didn't seem to be listening. She had her purse strap twisted around her wrist like a tourniquet. We found a spot way at the end of the parking lot. Quite a few parents were still unloading their kids' stuff. "I thought we'd be the last ones here," Mom said. "We got such a late start."

We each carried as much as we could manage into the East Tower. We had to wait forever for an elevator. "How are you going to get back and forth to class," Mom asked, "if you have to wait for the elevator every day?"

Christa adjusted the load of clothes in her arms. "It can't be this bad on a normal day. It's just because everybody's moving in and there are a lot of extra people around."

We finally got up to the tenth floor. There were kids Christa's age running all over the place, yelling to each other. Stereos blared three different songs into the hall. Frank raised his eyebrows. "I don't remember college being so noisy."

I felt like saying, "I bet you wrote on stones when you were in school," but I kept my mouth shut.

"Here it is," Christa said. "Ten-o-six."

The door was partly ajar. Christa swung it open the rest of the way. A tall girl with long blond hair jumped up. "Oh, hi. You must be Christa."

"That's me," Christa said. "Are you Bethany?"

She smiled. "Only on official documents. My friends call me Beth. Sorry about the mess. I haven't gotten everything put away yet. You just missed my parents. They left about half an hour ago."

I looked around the room. There wasn't an inch of

space anywhere. There were piles of clothes all over the floor. Art supplies and books spilled out of cartons and a whole stack of paintings leaned against one of the dressers.

"I hope you don't mind the top bunk," Beth said. "I'm afraid of heights."

"That's okay," Christa said. "I can sleep anywhere."

"Here, we'll shove some of my stuff out of the way." Beth made a space in the middle of the floor by piling a few cartons on top of each other. "We don't have a closet. You can hang your clothes on that pole."

Beth's stuff took up at least three quarters of the rack. She tried to squish them together. "I hope you brought hangers. They only had a few. I'm afraid I used them all up."

Christa hung her armload of clothes on the rod. This was only the first load, and already it was crammed full.

"These rooms are awfully small for two people," Mom said, trying to find a place to stand.

"It'll be all right, Mom. Once we get our stuff put away, there'll be more space." Christa climbed over some cartons to get to the window. "Look at the view. Didn't I tell you it was great?"

I followed her, almost tripping on the cords from Beth's stereo. The lake stretched out in the distance, framed by hills on both sides. I could see the road we'd followed into town. The clouds on the horizon were beginning to turn pink underneath from the setting sun. If I lived in this room, I'd spend my whole time staring out the window. All I could see from my window at home was the Baldwins' garage roof.

It took three more trips to get all of Christa's stuff upstairs, and she had us take most of the last load back because there wasn't any room for it. Half of her clothes were still out in the hall.

"Do you two want to come out to dinner with us?" Mom asked. "We can come back afterwards and help you unpack."

Beth looked at Christa. "Dinner's just starting here. I told some of the girls down the hall I'd meet them in the dining hall. I said I'd bring you along if you were here yet, but if you'd rather go out . . ."

"I think I'll go with Beth, Mom," Christa said. "I don't need any more help. Classes don't start until Tuesday. We'll have all day tomorrow to get settled in."

Mom looked around the room. I thought she was going to cry. "Well, I don't know. I think you could use a hand with this."

"Really, Mom, it's fine." Christa steered Mom toward the door. "You guys go on. You must be tired, with the wedding and everything. I'll call you tomorrow."

Christa and Beth walked us out to the car. I gave Christa a good-bye hug and started to cry. "Hang in there, kid," she whispered. "Remember, I'm always here if you need me."

We got in the car and started out. As I looked back, Christa and Beth had joined a whole bunch of other kids. Christa turned around and waved once before she was swallowed up by the crowd.

"I hate leaving her like this," Mom said. "That room is smaller than the one she has by herself at home."

Frank reached over and patted Mom's shoulder. "She'll be all right. She has to grow up someday."

"I know, but it just looked so . . . confusing."

"Christa's used to confusing, Mom. She's lived her whole life with us, remember?" I turned around in the backseat so I could watch the campus for as long as possible. I counted up ten floors on East Tower and figured out which room was Christa's. I envied her. She was starting a whole new life. I guess I was too, but I wasn't so sure I was going to like mine. It would be seven long years before I could be on my own.

"I think we'd better stop for dinner," Frank said as we drove into town. "I don't know about you two, but I'm starved." He pulled into a fried-chicken restaurant. "This should be fast."

The meal wasn't much fun, because Mom started crying every time she tried to take a bite of food. "Christa's going to be fine," Frank said for about the tenth time. "I'll bet she's made half a dozen new friends already, and she's forgotten all about us."

Mom blew her nose. "That's not exactly comforting, Frank."

I glared at him as I ripped the meat from a drumstick with my teeth. He was partly right. The first thing I'd do when I went to college was forget about Frank.

I must have fallen asleep as soon as we started out again, because I missed the whole trip home. It was almost nine-fifteen when we pulled into our driveway. I ran into the kitchen and grabbed the phone. I had to call Carla and fill her in on what had happened today.

"You aren't planning on calling someone at this hour, are you?" Frank asked, coming in the back door.

"Just Carla. She won't mind."

Frank looked at his watch. "Well, all right. But after this, no phone calls after nine o'clock. I don't want you disturbing her family."

"I'm not disturbing them," I said. "They go to bed late."

"Natalie," Mom said. "Just make your call quickly."

I was steaming by the time I finished dialing. Carla answered on the first ring. "What took you so long?" she asked. "I've been calling and calling."

"Christa packed everything she owned. It took forever to get her stuff unloaded. Besides it was a rotten trip. Frank is such a jerk."

"What did he do now?"

"I'll be right over and tell you all about it," I said.

"Good, because I need to talk, too," Carla said. "Why don't you sleep over tonight?"

"Sure," I said. "I'm dying to get out of here. It's weird with Christa gone, and Frank makes me so mad. I'll be right there."

I hung up and ran into the living room. "Mom, Carla wants me to stay over."

"Okay, honey," Mom said.

I was halfway up the stairs when Frank asked, "Are you sure it's all right with her parents? It's rude to wait until the last minute."

I couldn't believe my ears. "We do this all the time," I said. "Carla sleeps over here. I sleep over there. We don't plan anything."

"Natalie," Mom said. "Please don't talk to your— don't talk to Frank like that."

"What were you going to say?" I gripped the stair railing. " 'Don't talk to your father like that?' Because he's not my father. And he doesn't get to boss me around, either."

Mom stood up. "Go up to your room, Natalie. We need to talk." Mom followed me upstairs and closed the door behind her. "I don't want you using that tone of voice with Frank ever again."

"But, Mom, what right does he have to boss me around?"

"I know Frank isn't your father, and I'm not sure how other people work out this situation. Maybe I was wrong to insist on having the wedding before

Christa left for school. It didn't give us a chance to talk over how things were going to change around here."

"I don't see why anything has to change. Frank doesn't have any say about what I do."

Mom put her hands on my shoulders. "Frank is a good person, Natalie. I want you to respect him."

"I'm not going to respect him if he's going to boss me around." I shook loose from her grip. "He has no right."

"Maybe you need a little bossing around, young lady. We've managed on our own for the past few years, but things have been, well, pretty chaotic. I'm trying to change that." She started to straighten up the stuff on the top of my dresser, then gave up and turned to me. "Give Carla a call and tell her you'll see her tomorrow."

"Aw, Mom, please? I need to talk to her. Besides, tomorrow's Labor Day, and school starts the day after that. This is our last chance for a sleepover until next Friday."

Mom looked as if she was weakening for a minute; then she shook her head. "No, Frank's right. We have to get more organized. We're all going to learn to plan ahead, even for little things like sleeping over." She gave me a kiss on the top of the head and went out.

She wanted planning ahead? I'd give her planning ahead. I called Carla and told her I couldn't come over until morning.

Then I tore a piece of paper out of my notebook, grabbed a pen and wrote this note.

Dear Mom, (and Frank)

I am *planning* to go to Carla's at approximately ten A.M. tomorrow. I will have lunch there and go to the Labor Day Parade with Carla's family. This *plan* has been approved by Carla's mother.

After spending the rest of the day at Carla's, I *plan* to be home for dinner.

I *plan* to go to the first day of school on Tuesday.

After I pass sixth grade, I *plan* to attend and pass all the other grades.

Seven years from now, when I graduate from high school, I *plan* to attend college—maybe Corinthia.

When I graduate from college, I *plan* to have an exciting and challenging career.

I *do not plan* to get married—ever!

Chapter Five

I gulped down my cereal in the morning. I carefully left the note in the middle of the kitchen table and ran all the way over to Carla's house before Mom and Frank were up.

Carla was in the treehouse, as usual, working on a new version of her rainbow nails. "I feel as if I just escaped from prison," I said. "Life with Frank is going to be a real drag. He thinks he can tell me what to do."

"He can," Carla said. "He's the adult."

"What difference does that make?"

Carla shrugged. "Simple. Adults make decisions. Kids have to go along with them."

"What's the matter with you? Is this the same Carla Ackerman who had a fit last spring when the principal decided it was okay for boys to wear short shorts to school but not girls? Is this the same Carla Ackerman who circulated a petition through the whole school

41

saying girls should be able to wear shorts if boys could?"

"Big deal," Carla said. "Now *nobody* can wear shorts to school. That's what happens when you mess with adults."

"So it didn't work out the way you wanted it to," I said. "At least the rule is fair now."

Carla started nibbling at her thumbnail. "Yeah, and every boy in the class hates me."

"So what," I said. "They hate me, too, and I never even wrote a petition. Watch out, you're getting nail polish on your lip. Blue nail polish."

"Rats!" Carla grabbed a piece of Kleenex and rubbed it across her mouth, smearing the blue.

"What was it you wanted to tell me?" I asked.

"Something's happened."

"What?"

Carla opened the bottle of polish remover and started cleaning off her thumbnail. "It's my father. He's probably being transferred to Cleveland. He told us Friday night when he got home from work."

"Cleveland? You can't move away."

"It's just like I was saying." Carla repainted her blue nail. "The adult decides to move, so the kid has to go along. It's not like I could tell him, 'You and Mom go on to Cleveland without me, Dad. I'll just stay here in the treehouse.' "

"Why didn't you tell me this on Saturday?" I asked.

"I was going to, but I forgot."

"Forgot! How could you forget something as important as moving away?"

Carla shrugged. "Okay, so I blocked it out."

I leaned back against the treehouse wall, feeling as if someone had just kicked me in the stomach. "When would you be leaving?"

Carla looked away. "As soon as he knows for sure, we'll put the house up for sale."

"I can't imagine anyone else living in your house. It wouldn't be right."

"Don't think about it," Carla said. "I'm not."

"How can you be so calm?" I yelled. "Aren't you upset about moving?"

"Why bother getting upset?" Carla's eyes glinted like metal when she looked at me. "It wouldn't do any good. It never does. This is the longest we've ever lived in one place. It was our sixth house. I don't want to talk about it anymore."

I watched in silence as Carla dug through our treasure box. She pulled out an old magazine and started flipping through the pages.

"You think the whole problem will go away if you don't talk about it?" I asked, finally.

Carla shrugged. "Who knows? It's worth a try. Why worry about something before it happens?"

Maybe Carla was right. We thought we might have to move a couple of times when Dad was thinking of taking another job. But in the end he'd decided to stay where we were, and things went back to normal. We'd always lived in the same house until the divorce, when Mom, Christa, and I moved to Rochester. Carla was right not to talk about moving. It probably would never happen.

When the noon whistle blew, we went into the house to make sandwiches, then climbed back up to the treehouse. It was just starting to rain. The roof was made of tin, and it sounded as if a hundred ants in tap shoes were dancing over our heads.

"The rain could mess up going to the Labor Day parade this afternoon," I said.

Carla squinted at the raindrops dripping off the leaves. "Who cares? It's always the same stupid stuff anyway—a bunch of fire trucks."

"You haven't forgotten Berna Jean Farber and the Innie majorettes?"

"Who wants to see them?" Carla mumbled.

"They'll be marching in the rain. All their perfect hairdos will get soggy."

A little bit of the old sparkle came back into Carla's eyes. "That might be worth seeing," she said. "Old perfect Berna Jean looking not so perfect. Let's go."

"I have to go home and get my poncho," I said. We climbed down the ladder and ran all the way to my house, dodging puddles. We were dripping wet when we got there.

Frank looked up from stretching a measuring tape across the kitchen wall. "You two will catch your death of cold. Grab some towels to dry off and find some dry clothes. You have something to fit Carla, don't you, Natalie?"

"Sure, but it's warm out," I said. "Our clothes will dry fast. Besides, we'll probably just get wet again when we go back to Carla's."

"And we'll probably just get soaked again at the parade," Carla added.

Frank raised his eyebrows. "You're not going to a parade in this weather, are you? Besides, they'll probably cancel it."

Mom came into the room. "Cancel the Labor Day parade? I doubt it. They'd have it in a blizzard."

Frank turned to Mom. "Don't you think it's a mistake for the girls to go out in the rain? They could get sick."

"Mom, I can't miss the parade. It's tradition!"

Mom looked out the window. "Maybe it will clear up in another hour. Our weather is always so changeable. Besides, Natalie's been out in the rain before. Children are hardier than you think, Frank."

Frank folded up the measuring tape and fastened it with a rubber band. "I thought you were planning to stay over at Carla's today."

"Well, excuse me," I said. "I should have called for an appointment to come home. How careless of me."

Mom ran her fingers through her hair. "Natalie . . ."

"I'm just grabbing my poncho and I'm out of here, Mom. We're going to miss the beginning of the parade if we don't get moving."

I got my stuff and we ran back to Carla's.

Mrs. Ackerman looked out of the window. "The rain is coming down in sheets. Count me out for the parade."

"Aw, Mom," Carla pleaded. "We have to go . . . please?"

"I didn't say you couldn't go. *I'm* just not stupid enough to go out in this weather." Mrs. Ackerman smiled. "Go work on your father. He's a real sucker for parades. Last time I saw him, he was in the garage."

Carla's father was climbing into his yellow rubber fishing suit when we found him. "You girls ready?" he asked. "We don't want to miss the first band."

Good old Mr. Ackerman. You could always count on him. Carla and I piled into the backseat of the car, and we headed for the center of town. Mr. Ackerman turned the windshield wipers up to their highest speed, but it was still hard to see. "Can't understand why your mother lets a little rain get in her way," he said. "If you dress for the weather, you hardly notice it."

"Mom isn't a parade freak like you are, Dad. If we were going to a baseball game, she'd be driving and you'd be home."

Mr. Ackerman looked at Carla in the rearview mirror. "Your mother would *walk* in the rain to a baseball game if she had to. I'm sure she'll be at every Cleveland Indians home game. She's ecstatic about moving to a city with a major league team."

Carla slumped down in her seat at the word "moving."

Mr. Ackerman raised up a little to catch her eye again, then looked back at the road just in time to avoid hitting a parked car. "You're going to like Cleveland, Carla. There's lots to do there."

"What difference does it make?" Carla mumbled. "We won't be there long enough to get bored, anyway." Neither of them said anything until we found a parking spot close to the beginning of the parade route and we got out.

"I hear the bands," Carla said, acting like herself again. "That's where Berna Jean will be. The majorettes always march right in front of the school band."

The street was lined with people holding umbrellas, as if the rain had sprouted a whole crop of multicolored mushrooms. Some clowns went by on bicycles, throwing candy to the kids. Carla and I didn't run after the candy. It wasn't cool to do that at our age. A few pieces landed right at our feet, though, so we picked them up.

The clouds were getting darker. "Here they come," Carla said.

In the distance we could see our school band with

the majorettes in the lead. Berna Jean's long blond hair was plastered flat against her head, and the skirt of her perky little red uniform hung around her legs like a soggy dish rag. The other three Innies, Adrian Brower, Kimberly Spitz, and Mavis Dittmar, marched behind her.

Carla laughed. "They look worse than we ever have. I wish I had a camera."

As they got right in front of us, Berna Jean gave the crowd one of her usual dazzling smiles and tossed her baton in the air. When she looked up to catch it, the rain was coming down so hard, she couldn't keep her eyes open. The silver baton almost disappeared for a second in a solid sheet of water. Then it spun back into view and bopped her right on the nose. The baton bounced a few times on the pavement and rolled over to us. Carla and I stood motionless as Berna Jean came over to grab it.

"Nice catch," Carla said. "You must have practiced for hours to get the baton to land on your nose like that."

Berna Jean glared at us with blood dripping down her upper lip, then ran back to her spot and kept marching.

"She's going to get you for that," I said as the band moved past us. The tuba was so waterlogged, it was making gurgling sounds instead of music.

Carla grinned. "I don't care. Berna Jean and her

group are always nasty to us anyway. What's she going to do, shoot me?"

"Probably not, but I wouldn't be surprised if she clunked you on the nose with her trusty baton."

After all of the bands and fire trucks had passed, regular traffic was going by. "Come on, Dad," Carla said. "It's over. Let's get out of here."

Mr. Ackerman held up his hand, straining to see down the street. "You can never tell. Sometimes a few cars slip in between parade units. There might be another band back there."

"That's not a few cars, Dad. It's a few hundred."

Mr. Ackerman finally gave up, and we made a dash for the car. Carla and I laughed about the dripping Innies all the way back to her house.

We went up to her room, and I borrowed some dry clothes. Carla did a great imitation of Berna Jean getting clobbered with her baton. Then she staggered across the room, clutching her nose. "I'm fine," she said in Berna Jean's husky voice. "The show must go on. Just have one of the ambulances ready to give me a transfusion at the end of the parade route."

We collapsed on Carla's bed, laughing. Then she suddenly got quiet.

"What's the matter?" I asked, propping myself up on one elbow.

"I was just thinking. That might be the last time I ever see Berna Jean march in the Labor Day parade."

"Don't be silly. A little bloody nose isn't going to keep Berna Jean away from parades."

"No, but moving to Cleveland is going to keep me away."

"Oh," I said. "I forgot." I really had forgotten. I just wasn't ready to admit that my best friend—my only friend—might be moving away for good. Christa had left me to go off to college, and though Mom was still living at home, all she could think about was Frank. Now Carla might be deserting me, too. It wasn't fair.

Chapter Six

I sat on the front steps the next morning, waiting for Carla. I could spot her rainbow nails half a block away. She also noticed I wasn't wearing mine.

"What did you do?" she asked, coming up our front walk. "Chicken out?"

"I decided they didn't go with my outfit," I said.

Carla sat next to me on the steps. "Well, thanks a bunch. Now I'm going to go in alone like this and look like an idiot? I bet Frank wouldn't let you, would he?"

"It didn't have anything to do with Frank. I just decided I didn't want to do it."

"You couldn't call me," Carla asked, "and let me know?"

I shrugged. "No. Frank won't let me make any calls after nine. If you want to take off the nail polish, you can come in the house. We're still early for school."

Carla stood and whipped her backpack up on her shoulder. "Forget it. If you want to be an individual, you have to look like one. I'm not afraid to go to school like this. I think it looks neat." She turned and started down the sidewalk.

I followed her. "You're absolutely right. I'm going to wear rainbow nails tomorrow." I had to run a few steps to catch up because she was walking much faster than usual. "Aren't you glad we're in class together again this year?" I asked. "I wonder who else will be with us?"

Carla shrugged. "Who knows? Who cares?"

"I just don't want to get stuck with the Innies," I said. All four Innies had been in our class two years ago. Then last year we didn't have any of them, so we only had to put up with them in the lunchroom, gym, and chorus.

We walked along in silence. I could tell Carla was mad at me about the rainbow nails. Usually we talked nonstop all the way to school—especially on the first day. I always got nervous about the beginning of the school year. Mrs. Buckley, our teacher, was supposed to be nice, but you never could be sure about what other kids told you. Miss Simkewicz, our last year's teacher, was supposed to be nice, too. She turned out to be mean right down to her bones.

The school buses were lined up in the circular drive-way in front of the school when we got there. We lived just inside the one-mile limit, so we had to walk. I was glad, in a way. The kids in the block beyond Carla were on the bus for almost an hour because they got picked up first and had to drive for miles to get the other kids.

I followed Carla down the hall to room 104. "Oh great," Carla muttered. "Look who we got."

Berna Jean was sitting in one of the front seats, with Mavis on one side of her and Kimberly on the other. Adrian wasn't there.

"Three out of four Innies," I whispered. "How did we get so lucky?"

I tried to slip past them to a seat in the back, but Carla stopped at Berna Jean's desk. "You changed your hair, Berna Jean," she said. "I liked the way it looked yesterday in the parade."

Berna Jean tossed her hair over her shoulder. "At least I get out and do something useful, which is more than some people I could mention. And speaking of appearances, what on earth have you done to your fingernails?"

"These just happen to be rainbow nails," Carla said, holding them up for everybody to see. "It's the latest thing. I'm surprised you didn't know about it."

A slow smile spread over Berna Jean's face. "The latest thing? I saw those a couple of years ago in a magazine. I thought they looked stupid." She glanced back at Carla's nails. "They still do."

Carla's face turned red as some of the kids started to laugh. She wrapped her arms tight around her backpack, hiding her fingers.

I went over to stand next to Carla. "I think rainbow

nails look great," I said. "I had them too, but I changed my mind for today because they didn't match my outfit. I'll wear them tomorrow, though."

Kimberly snorted. "Your outfit? Nothing would match that mess."

Carla started to say something, but the bell rang. I grabbed her arm and pulled her down the aisle to a couple of seats in the back.

Mrs. Buckley looked up from her desk. "All right, class. Let's get started. I have a seating chart in alphabetical order."

The Innies groaned. That meant they wouldn't be able to sit together.

Mrs. Buckley had us all line up against the walls. Then she moved down the rows of desks, stopping at each one to call out a name. Ackerman was the first name to be called, so Carla had to sit right in front of Anthony Argento. He slouched down in his seat and stretched out so he could tap his foot against the leg of Carla's chair. When she turned around to glare at him, he just grinned and kept on tapping.

I thought I might be in the row next to Carla, but there were too many C's and D's. Berna Jean Farber was called for the third row. Then the alphabet did a major jump, and my name was called to sit behind her. By the time Mrs. Buckley finished her list, I was surrounded. Not only did I have Berna Jean Farber in front of me, but Mavis Dittmar was on my right and Kimberly Spitz on my left.

They spent most of the morning passing notes to each other. Berna Jean passed a note to Mavis, then Mavis glanced at me and laughed. Mavis wrote something and sent the note back to Berna Jean. Berna Jean turned around to look at me, then nodded to Mavis and they both started giggling. Soon the note made its way to Kimberly, and she had the same reaction. I pretended not to notice what was going on, but I could feel my face getting red.

I could hardly wait for lunch so I could talk to Carla. She'd make fun of the Innies, and I'd feel better again. What would I do if Carla moved? School would be unbearable.

Finally the lunch bell rang. Carla slipped out of the room right away, but waited for me in the hall. "If Anthony doesn't stop using my chair leg to practice drum beats, I'm going to go nuts."

"You think you have problems. At least you're not surrounded by Innies." I told her about the note-passing after we found a table.

"Don't pay any attention to them," Carla said. "They'll stop doing it if you don't get upset over it."

"Maybe they'd leave us alone if you'd stop challenging Berna Jean all the time."

Carla fished her lunch bag out of her backpack. "I just like to get to her before she gets to me. You can't let people like that have the upper hand."

"Shhh!" I said. "Here they come." I could see Berna Jean and the Innies making their way across the cafeteria. Adrian was back with them, and some other kids were trailing along, trying to get noticed.

"You know what the Innies remind me of?" Carla said. "Remember when we went to the Renaissance Faire last summer?"

I watched them for a few seconds, then laughed. "You're right! It's just like when Queen Elizabeth and her court come through the Faire. Everybody stops what they're doing and gets swept along with them."

I couldn't tell whether she heard us or not, but Berna Jean came over to our table and stopped. "By the way, Natalie, I heard your mother's wedding was very interesting. My parents were there, you know. Daddy works at the same bank as your new stepfather."

"Big deal," I mumbled.

"I hear you got a little carried away during the ceremony, Natalie." Berna Jean leaned on our table. Her long blond hair practically swung into my face. "I hear you got confused and thought you were the bride."

This couldn't be happening. Berna Jean couldn't possibly be telling the entire world about me throwing the bouquet at Mom's wedding. I hadn't even told Carla about that. As a matter of fact, I'd blocked the whole wedding out of my mind until Berna Jean had to bring it up.

That's when I figured it out. This had to be a dream—one of those night-before-the-first-day-of-school-jitters nightmares. Any minute my alarm clock would go off, and I'd get up and get dressed for school. This time I'd leave the rainbow nails on so Carla wouldn't get mad at me. That was the great part about dreams. They gave you a chance to fix your mistakes before they really happened.

I realized Berna Jean had delivered her punch line, and all the kids who had gathered around were laughing. "Fat chance of Natalie Hanson ever becoming a bride," Mavis hooted.

Berna Jean gave a Queen Elizabeth gesture with her hand, and they all moved on to a table near the end of the cafeteria.

"You didn't really, did you?" Carla whispered, her eyes wide.

"I didn't what?"

"Throw the bouquet."

"It was an accident."

"Berna Jean didn't make it sound like an accident. What was the matter with you?"

"Look, " I said, "this is *my* dream, so stop criticizing me."

Carla gripped my shoulder. "Natalie, you're talking weird. What do you mean it's your dream?"

"When I wake up, which I'm going to do any second, this will all be over." I looked around the cafeteria. Everything seemed so real, not like most dreams, where things aren't quite the way they are in real life. "Carla . . . this is a dream, isn't it?"

"If it is, we're both having it at the same time."

I put my head down on the table, a very real, un-dreamlike cafeteria table. "I'm ruined."

Carla poked me with her elbow. "I told you before. Don't let them see that they upset you. Laugh."

"Laugh? About what?"

"Not about anything. Just laugh. Pretend I just said something funny."

"Heh heh heh. That's the best I can do. That crying on the inside, laughing on the outside stuff doesn't work for me."

Carla threw her head back and laughed so loud you could probably hear it all the way down in the main office. "Natalie Hanson, you say the funniest things. You'd better not let Berna Jean hear that one."

We took turns laughing for a few minutes, but the Innies didn't seem to be noticing us. A few other kids were giving us strange looks, though. "I wonder why the Innies pick on us?" I asked.

Carla sat up straight. "Because we're different, that's why. We don't fit into any of the other groups, and that bugs them."

I wadded up my garbage and shoved it back into my lunch bag. "Maybe we should just become nerds. Then they'd leave us alone."

"Don't you even think of doing that, Natalie Hanson." Carla slapped her hand down on the table. "This year *we're* going to be the in group. People will be falling all over themselves trying to join us."

"Yeah? And what happens if you move? Where does that leave me?"

Carla scrunched the rest of her sandwich in her napkin. "I told you. We're not going to think about that until it happens." She was quiet for a few minutes, staring at the crumpled napkin on the table. Then she looked up. "Thanks for sticking up for me when Berna Jean was teasing me about the rainbow nails."

I shrugged. "What are friends for?"

I thought about that when we got back to class. There I was, surrounded by Innies on three sides. Then Carla turned around from her seat up front and winked at me.

That's what friends are for. They're for making you feel you're not alone. And as long as Carla stayed around, I wouldn't be.

Chapter Seven

Carla's mother picked her up after school for a dentist's appointment, so I had to walk home alone. A truck from Netzman's appliance store was just pulling out of our driveway when I turned onto our street.

"What did we get, Mom?" I asked, bursting into the kitchen. "Is it a new TV?" Our old TV had only three channels, and one of them flipped constantly.

"No, honey. It's a stove. Isn't it a beauty?"

I wasn't used to having Mom say "Isn't it a beauty?" about things like stoves.

Mom ran her hand over the shiny white surface. "This is a wedding present from Frank. Now I can cook some real meals."

"Great," I said. "I hope this thing does the grocery shopping, too." Mom always ran to the corner store before dinner to grab something to zap in the microwave.

"Don't be sarcastic, Natalie. Frank got me some new

cookbooks, too, and a notebook of his mother's favorite recipes. I've started the shopping list for dinner."

I picked up the list from the table. "Oregano, mar . . . marjoram? What is this stuff, anyway?"

Mom was busy pulling little bottles and tin boxes out of the corner cupboard. "They're herbs and spices. Frank's mother says they don't keep well—especially the herbs. Mine must be years old. She said you can test them by shaking them out on a paper towel. If some of the little leaves seem to be crawling away, it means they're infested with bugs." She shook something called thyme on a paper towel, and half of the little flecks took off across the counter.

"Looks like the thyme is past its prime," I said. "You haven't been feeding us this stuff, have you?"

Mom smiled. "No, thank heaven. I never did know how to use herbs."

I traced my finger down to the end of the grocery list. "Is there anything here you can actually eat?"

"I'm making a special spaghetti sauce—Frank's mother's recipe. She's a marvelous cook, you know."

"How do you know? Did you ever eat anything she cooked?"

Mom swept the old tins and bottles off the counter into a garbage bag. "Well no, but Frank raves about her meals."

"Frank raves about everything that's different from the way we do things."

"Natalie, that's not true. He's just trying to help me be more organized. I'm grateful, really."

Just then we heard Frank's car in the driveway. A big smile broke across his face when he came in and saw the stove. He set a large bag down on the kitchen table. "Ah, they delivered it. Have you tried it out?"

Mom hugged him. "Everything works. I'm planning a gourmet meal for supper—your mother's spaghetti sauce."

"Terrific. I'll help you. I know some of the little tricks Mother probably didn't put in the recipe. She tends to guard her secrets."

"After I have some practice," Mom said, "I'd like to have her over for dinner. I want her to see I'm not a hopeless disaster in the kitchen."

Frank kissed her. "You're not a disaster at anything."

I turned away and started squashing the little bugs on the counter with my fingernail It made me feel weird when Frank and Mom got all lovey-dovey.

Frank went over to the stove and ran his hand over the shiny surface. "This sure is a beauty. I'm glad we went for the top-of-the-line model. This stove can do just about anything."

"Yeah?" I said. "Can it wake you up in the morning?"

Frank grinned. "Now, I'm glad you asked that, young lady. It just so happens this amazing stove can do exactly that—with a little help from this." He opened the bag on the table and pulled out a large box.

"Oh, Frank," Mom said. "An automatic coffee maker. I've never had one."

Frank set up the coffee maker on the counter right next to the stove. "We'll fill this each night and plug it into the timer on the stove. Then we can wake up every morning to the aroma of fresh coffee."

"That's not going to wake anybody up," I said.

Frank gave the coffee maker a little tap. "Sure it will. Haven't you seen all those commercials on TV?"

"I think it's great," Mom said. "It's like having a maid make breakfast while you're still in bed." This time she kissed him.

I had to get out of there. "I'm going down to Carla's," I said. "I'll be back in time for dinner."

Mom stopped kissing Frank just long enough to say, "Okay, honey."

When I got to Carla's house, there was a For Sale sign out front. Carla's moving wasn't something that would go away if we didn't talk about it. It was really happening. I was about to ring the doorbell when I realized the car wasn't in the garage. I'd forgotten about Carla's dentist appointment.

I climbed up to the treehouse where I had a good view of the For Sale sign. I sat for a long time, staring at the sign, trying to make myself believe what was happening. Finally, I climbed down and headed for home.

There was a strange car in our driveway.

"Look who came to visit, Natalie," Mom said as I came into the living room.

Mrs. Willderby sat on Dad's old reclining chair, her back straight as a broom handle. She looked as if she were afraid the stains on the covering of the chair would transfer to her light blue dress. Mom had been talking for years about having the living room furniture recovered, but hadn't gotten around to it. You don't notice things like stained furniture until somebody like Mrs. Willderby comes for a visit.

"Hi," I mumbled, trying to back toward the stairs. Mrs. Willderby's sharp little eyes gave me the once-over, as if she expected me to curtsy or something.

Mom's smile was too bright to be real. "Mother Willderby dropped by just in time for dinner. Isn't that nice?"

"Sure," I said. What was the matter with everybody? Mom and Frank sat on the couch. They both looked like store mannequins that somebody had put together wrong—as if they had their right arms in their left arm sockets.

Mom stood up suddenly. "Natalie, I could use your help in the kitchen."

Frank jumped to his feet. "I really wish you'd let me help, Anne."

"Never mind, Frank," Mom said. "You just relax and talk with your mother. Natalie and I will get dinner on."

Mrs. Willderby beamed. "Anne is exactly right. I'm so glad to see that Natalie is learning domestic skills. Why, when I was her age, I prepared all the family meals by myself. My mother wasn't well, you know."

"That's a shame," Mom said, yanking me into the kitchen. She pulled the door shut behind us and leaned on it, her eyes closed. "I don't believe that woman came here unannounced," she whispered. "I was going to invite her for dinner but not until I had a chance to get my act together."

"Mom," I said, "something awful's happened."

Mom opened her eyes. "Something worse than having Mrs. Willderby show up for dinner?"

"Much worse. Carla's moving. She told me the other day, but I thought it wouldn't happen. I was over there just now, and there's a For Sale sign in front of her house."

Just then one of the big pots on the stove started to boil over. Mom grabbed a couple of potholders and poured the contents of the pot into a strainer in the sink. Her head disappeared for a second in a cloud of steam. "That's a shame about Carla, honey. We'll have to talk about it when things aren't quite so hectic. This is much harder to do than the stuff in the little cans with the sauce already on the spaghetti." She turned suddenly. "Oh! The sauce! Stir that pot on the stove for a minute, will you, Natalie? I think we'll dish up the plates in here and carry them into the dining room. We don't really have any decent serving dishes."

I stirred the sauce as the bubbles kept forming and bursting, like the lava in the volcano movie we'd seen in science class. Mom didn't care that my whole life was falling apart. All she cared about was impressing Frank and his mother. I was getting sort of hypnotized by the plopping sound of the simmering sauce when I noticed something. "Are you supposed to have big hunks of black stuff in here, Mom?"

"What black stuff?" Mom pushed the steam-dampened curls from her eyes and peered into the sauce pot. "Rats! I had the heat turned up too high. The sauce must have burned on the bottom." She took a spoonful of sauce, blew on it, and then tasted it. She shivered. "It's awful. Now what do I do?"

"I think Carla's mom puts vinegar in when something burns."

Mom grabbed the vinegar bottle from the cupboard and dumped some in. She stirred it, then tasted again. "It's even worse. How much of this am I supposed to use?"

"I don't know. I'll call Carla and ask."

"Hi, it's me," I said when I heard her voice.

"Who's me?" she asked.

"Come off it, Carla. It's Natalie. How was your dentist's appointment?"

"How is any dentist's appointment? Gruesome. What do you want?"

"Mom and I have a cooking disaster here. Remember when your mom burned the potatoes last month? Didn't she use vinegar?"

"Yeah, to clean out the pot."

"But it doesn't help the taste?"

Carla laughed. "Are you kidding? She threw out the potatoes."

"Oh yeah, I forgot. Thanks, Carla."

Mom was spooning little black hunks out of the sauce with a teaspoon. "What's the verdict? Did I use too much vinegar? Is that why it tastes so sour?"

"I guess so. Maybe we could just send out for pizza."

"I can't do that, Natalie. Frank's mother already thinks I'm incompetent. That would convince her. I'm just going to sweeten up this sauce." She dumped a whole bowl of sugar into the pot, then tasted it. "Hmm. Not exactly like spaghetti sauce, but it isn't bad."

She dipped the spoon in again and held it out to me. "What do you think?"

I tasted it. "You're right. It's definitely not spaghetti sauce." I couldn't believe she was actually going to serve this.

"Natalie, dish some spaghetti onto a plate and bring it over here for sauce."

I went to the sink with a plate. The spaghetti had formed into one solid mass, like a sculpture of a worm family reunion. "Mom, aren't these supposed to be in separate pieces?" I asked.

"Natalie!" Mom came up behind me. "Don't make jokes at a time like this." She plunged her fork into the quivering blob of noodles. "What have you done to my spaghetti?"

"I didn't do anything. It's all kind of glued together."

"Maybe we could just slice it apart with a knife," Mom said.

"Great idea, Mom. I can see it all now. Here, Mrs. Willderby, have a slice of spaghetti."

Mom paced back and forth across the kitchen. "I've got it. The blender." She shoved the blob into the blender and turned it on. "This should separate those little devils," she said.

The blender made a low growling sound for about half a minute, then smoke came out of its base. Mom yanked the plug from the wall. "Now what do we do?"

Suddenly Frank burst into the kitchen. Mrs. Willderby was right behind him. "I smell smoke!" Frank said. "Is something wrong?"

"Nothing to worry about," I said. "Another electrical appliance just bit the dust."

Frank peered into the blender. "What . . . what is this?"

Mom was standing over the sink. From the way her shoulders were shaking, I could tell she was crying.

"It's blender spaghetti," I said. "A new recipe. You're going to love it. Well, you would have loved it, except the blender conked out. So now we can't finish it. Anybody want to order out for pizza?"

Mrs. Willderby was standing by the sauce pot, watching the black hunks surface and disappear into the red goop. Her nostrils flared as she caught a whiff of the vinegar. "Pizza sounds like a fine idea to me," she said.

Frank steered his mother out of the kitchen. "I'll call right now and order it."

Mom turned around as soon as she heard the kitchen door close. Her face was streaked with tears. "Well, did I make a mess of that or what?"

I put my arms around her. "Don't worry, Mom. At least one good thing will come of this."

"What's that?"

"Mrs. Willderby will think twice before she drops in for dinner again."

Chapter Eight

I was right about Mrs. Willderby not wanting to come over to eat at our house again. But that didn't solve our problem. The next night, she invited us to *her* house for dinner.

"Do I have to go, Mom? I really need to see Carla tonight."

"You spend most of your waking hours with Carla," Mom said. "You can spend tonight with us."

"But you don't understand. Carla acted really funny at school when I asked her about the sign in front of her house. She hardly talked to me all day."

"It's an early dinner, Natalie. Maybe we'll get home in time for you to see Carla afterward. It wouldn't be polite for you to refuse Mrs. Willderby's invitation. She's family now. Go upstairs and change into something more presentable."

I grabbed my books from the kitchen table. "If I'm presentable enough for school and Carla, I'm presentable enough for Mrs. Willderby."

Mom sighed. "Don't be difficult, honey. You know how Frank's mother is."

"I sure do. That's why I want to stay home. Why is it whenever a kid has plans, they don't count?"

Mrs. Willderby's house looked like something out of a magazine. All of the furniture matched, as if she had bought it in a set, not one piece at a time on sale, the way Mom did. The rugs were so thick and squishy I wasn't sure whether I was supposed to step on them or not. I was making my way around the edge of the living room when I noticed both Frank and Mrs. Willderby walking on the rug, so I did, too.

"I'm *sooo* glad you could come over this evening," Mrs. Willderby said. She had a funny way of jutting her chin in and out when she talked. The loose skin on her throat jiggled like a chicken's wattles. "I've been anxious to get to know little Natalie better. Let me look at you, dear."

Mrs. Willderby motioned for me to turn around. When I had my back to her, I made a face at Mom.

"Yes, yes," Mrs. Willderby said. "I think I have just the thing for you. Come on upstairs with me, Natalie."

I turned to Mom for help, but she just nodded and smiled, so I didn't have any choice but to follow Mrs. Willderby up the wide, curving staircase. She went into a bedroom and opened a closet that was almost as big as my room at home. There was a wooden chest against one wall of the closet. When she lifted the lid, the smell of mothballs filled the room. "I've been saving this for years. I thought I might have a daughter some day, but of course I just had Frank."

She pulled a dark red, blue, and green plaid kilt from the trunk. "This was our family dress tartan," she said, holding it up. "I was a Lindsay. My family was from Scotland."

"That's nice," I mumbled, wondering how soon I could make my escape.

"Here," she said, handing me the kilt. "Try it on. I'm sure you're about the same size I was at your age. I want you to have it."

She wanted me to put on some old thing she wore as a kid? "Gee, thanks," I said, "but I couldn't take it. It must have sentimental value."

"Nonsense." Mrs. Willderby pushed me into a small room off the bedroom. "Go into the dressing room and try it on." She closed the door behind me. There were mirrors on two walls and a vanity across the back. I took off my jeans and wrapped the kilt around my waist, fastening the little leather straps and buckles. It had about a million pleats.

I could hear Mom's voice in the bedroom. "Come on out, Natalie. Let's see how you look."

Mrs. Willderby beamed when I opened the door. "I knew it. It's a perfect fit. Twirl around, Natalie, so your mother can see how beautifully the pleats fall."

I didn't twirl. I just glared at Mom.

"It's a lovely skirt," Mom said. "It's an authentic kilt from Scotland, honey."

Mrs. Willderby smiled and patted me on the head. "Why don't you keep it on for dinner, dear? I have to run downstairs and check on the roast." She turned at the head of the stairs. "I do think it's so nice to see young people in skirts, don't you?" She gave a disapproving glance at Mom's slacks and headed down the stairs.

"Mom," I whispered. "I'm not going to wear this thing. It's older than both of us put together, and it stinks of mothballs."

Mom raked her fingers through her hair. "I know how you feel, honey, but you should be honored that she wants to give it to you. You can tell how much it means to her."

"That's a bunch of baloney. She just didn't want me coming to dinner in jeans. She'll probably be up here any minute digging out some old dress for you to put on."

Mom looked in the mirror, smoothing her bulky sweater down over her slacks. "I should have put on something dressier."

"Why? You look nice. You're not going to let Mrs. Willderby start telling you how to dress, are you? I know *I'm* not." I undid the kilt's buckles and took it off. "This thing itches like crazy." I folded it on the bed and put my jeans back on.

I saw the disapproval on Mrs. Willderby's face as Mom and I came back down the stairs, but all she said was "Dinner's ready."

The meal was a nightmare. It was like a silverware exam that Mrs. Willderby concocted to make Mom and me look stupid. We each had so many forks and spoons we could have set the table for ten more people. I guess it was important which one you picked up first. Mrs. Willderby made a big deal out of teaching me, but I know she noticed Mom didn't have any idea what to do either. Every time I picked up the wrong fork, Mrs. Willderby would reach over and tap my hand, then smile and show me which one I was supposed to be using.

"They all look alike to me," I said. "What difference does it make which one you use?"

I felt Mom trying to kick me under the table, but she missed.

"A lady should know the difference," Mrs. Willderby said. "You may be in a situation someday where it's important."

I wanted to say I'd never be coming back *here* again, but I kept my mouth shut. I had the feeling anything I said could get Mom in as much trouble as me.

The meal was weird. We started with raw oysters. Mrs. Willderby and Frank swallowed them whole. I almost threw up just watching them. I refused to even look at the slimy little things. Mom tried one. It was two or three minutes before she actually managed to swallow it, and when she did, she looked green.

By the time we finally got home, it was too late to go over to Carla's. It was too late even to call her, thanks to Frank's "no calls after nine o'clock" rule. At least we'd set up plans for me to sleep over Friday night, so I had something to look forward to.

I had a feeling something was wrong the next morning when Carla showed up.

"Everything's all set for me to stay over at your house tonight," I said. "I think I've figured out the secret for getting around Frank. As long as I plan something at least twenty-four hours in advance, it's okay with him."

Carla didn't say anything. She just kept walking.

I ran a couple of steps to catch up. "I'm supposed to come for dinner, right?"

Carla stared straight ahead. "I guess so. If you feel like it."

"What do you mean? Of course I feel like it, but not if you're going to act like a pill. Do you want me to come over or not?"

"Sure," Carla said, still not looking at me. "It's just hard to know what I want lately. We've already had people coming through the house. I hate having strangers looking into my closet." She was walking faster, almost running.

"Maybe nobody will like your house," I said. "Then it won't sell, and you'll have to stay."

"Yeah, right!" Carla ran up the front steps to the school and disappeared before I could catch up.

That night at dinner, Mrs. Ackerman served beef stew with dumplings. "Want another helping, Natalie?" she asked.

"You bet," I said. "You know it's my favorite meal." I thought about never having it again if the Ackermans moved away. "Could you give my mom the recipe?"

Mrs. Ackerman ladled more stew into my bowl. "I don't really have a recipe, Nat. I always start out with hunks of beef, but then I put in just about anything that happens to be in the refrigerator."

I pictured our refrigerator, with half of the food growing little fuzzy sweaters, and decided not to pass the recipe along to Mom.

Carla barely ate anything, even though it was her second-favorite meal, and she didn't talk much during dinner. Mrs. Ackerman made up for Carla's silence by giving us a play-by-play description of the last Cleveland Indians game.

After dinner we went back to the treehouse. Carla just kept staring off into space and yawning a lot.

"You want to do something?" I asked.

"Like what?"

"I don't know. We could see what's on TV or walk down to the corner store for ice cream cones. I have my allowance money."

Carla shrugged. "I don't care. I don't really feel like doing anything."

I wasn't used to seeing Carla like this. She was usually the one with all the ideas. Now she sat in silence, shuffling through the things in our treasure box. "Do you want me to go home instead of sleeping over?" I asked finally.

She didn't even look up. "Suit yourself."

"I guess I'll go then, if you don't care whether I stay or not." I figured that would snap her out of her mood and she'd beg me to stay.

"Okay, see you," Carla said, still not looking at me. She didn't even seem disappointed that I was leaving.

I climbed down the first couple of steps, then stopped, my chin even with the floor. "Knock off with the silent treatment, Carla. You think you're the only one who's upset about your moving? How do you think I feel?"

Carla looked at me for the first time, but she still didn't say anything.

"And that's not all I'm upset about, either," I said. "With Christa gone, I'm left with Mom and Frank. Since all Mom cares about these days is Frank, that leaves just me. And now you'll barely speak to me anymore, so I'm really alone." I climbed down a couple more steps and pressed my forehead into a ladder rung, trying to keep the tears from coming.

I felt a tap on my shoulder. Carla was looking down through the hole in the treehouse floor. "I'm sorry," she said. "I was feeling alone, too. Dad's excited about his new job, and Mom can't wait to see an Indians game. I'm the only one around here who doesn't talk about Cleveland from morning to night."

"Maybe the whole thing will fall through," I said, climbing back through the opening. "The Bensons down the street have been trying to sell their house for months."

"That's just it," Carla said. "We might not have to wait for the house to sell. Since Dad's company wants him to transfer, they might take care of moving all our stuff and selling the house. We could leave as soon as Dad finds a house for us in Cleveland. Then Mom and Dad would just have to come back and sign some papers when our house here is sold."

My stomach tightened into a knot. "I don't understand. What's the big rush?"

Carla shrugged. "Mom and Dad want me to get into my new school as soon as possible, so I can 'adjust more easily.' Boy, am I ever sick of adjusting."

"You'll make new friends," I said.

"Who wants to?" Carla's eyes were glassy with tears.

"It's always like this. We move to a new place, and I meet somebody I think is going to be my friend for life. Then, just when I'm starting to feel as if I belong, we have to pack up and go again. I've learned to ease off on a friendship at the end. That way the leaving doesn't hurt as much."

"That's why you were acting the way you did?"

Carla nodded. "I was trying to pretend we weren't friends."

"But we are friends," I said, "best friends. That's not going to change just because you move away. We can write letters, and maybe we can even visit each other sometimes."

"It doesn't work." Carla leaned on the railing of the treehouse, looking out over her yard. "Everybody makes promises, but nobody ever writes. Maybe I get a few letters, but then they forget. I forget too." She shrugged. "That's life."

"I'll write forever and ever," I said. "I'm not like those other friends of yours."

"That's what you say now. Just wait a few months."

"No, really," I said. "I'm a great letter writer. I even write to my grandmother, and it's hard to think of things to tell her. With you, I'd have a hundred things a day to write about."

"Maybe you are different," Carla said. "Come on. Let's go get those ice cream cones."

"Okay," I said. "But promise me one thing."

"What's that?"

"Let's spend as much time together as we possibly can before you leave. No more easing off on our friendship."

Carla looked at me for a few seconds, then smiled. "Okay. We'll try it your way."

Chapter Nine

Carla and I spent more time with each other that next week than we had in the past month. When we weren't together, we were talking on the phone. We didn't avoid mentioning her moving anymore. Instead, we made plans for visiting each other. We even asked the phone company how much it would cost to call each other long distance. We found out that late-night phone calls were the cheapest, so we could afford to talk for fifteen or twenty minutes each time.

Carla spent the next weekend with us because her mother was flying out to Cleveland to look at a house. Her mother dropped her off Friday night on the way to the airport.

"Don't you want to help pick out your new house?" I asked, when we went up to my room.

Carla shrugged. "Who cares? I probably won't be there long enough to get used to it." She reached in her pocket. "Here, I got the calendars to mark down our phone schedule. They were free at the card shop."

"Friday nights will be the best," I said.

Carla nodded. "I know my Mom wouldn't let me call after eleven on a school night. Is Frank going to give you a problem?"

"No, I explained what we were doing, each calling every other week. He and Mom both said it's okay."

We marked all the Fridays in September, October, and November with "C" for Carla and "N" for me. Carla flipped to the last page of her calendar. "I get the first and third weeks of December and you get the second and fourth. That takes care of this year. We'll have to get new calendars when these run out."

We spent the next couple of hours making plans to visit each other next summer. We'd both save money from our allowances to put toward plane fare for one of us. We'd decide later which one of us would get to fly. I felt much better when I went to sleep that night. Even if Carla moved away, we'd still be best friends.

The doorbell rang so early Saturday morning, Frank's coffeepot hadn't even turned itself on yet. I pulled the covers up over my head, but Mom and Frank didn't seem to be waking up. Carla slept right through it, too, but the nagging sound of the bell was making me nuts. I threw on my robe and went down to the front door.

It was Mrs. Willderby. "Goodness," she said, "I had no idea you people slept so late. You're missing the best part of the day."

"It's Saturday," I said. "We sleep in on Saturdays."

"Well, surely, you've slept enough." Mrs. Willderby pushed her way past me. "Call my son and your mother, dear."

I didn't have to call them because when I turned around, Mom and Frank were coming down the stairs. Frank was tying the sash of his bathrobe. "Mother," he said, "you're certainly up bright and early."

"Which is more than I can say for some people around here." Mrs. Willderby marched into the living room. "You two wake up, because we have a lot of work to do today."

"What kind of work?" I asked.

Mrs. Willderby did a little twirl, waving her arm around the living room like a fairy godmother. Well, somebody smaller might have looked like a fairy godmother. Mrs. Willderby looked like a hen flapping her wings. "We're going to transform this room. It will be my gift to you."

"Mother Willderby," Mom said. "That's really not necessary."

Mrs. Willderby waved her away. "Nonsense! Nonsense! I've called my decorator, and she's meeting me here at nine." She glanced at her watch. "Good heavens, that's any minute. Run upstairs, everybody, and get dressed."

The three of us stumbled back up the stairs. Mrs. Willderby was the kind of person that—well, when she ordered you to do something, you did it without thinking. Especially if you were half asleep.

Before we could get ready, the doorbell rang again. I could hear Mrs. Willderby letting somebody in. I left Carla still sleeping in my room and got back downstairs before Mom and Frank. Mrs. Willderby was talking to a woman with blond hair that draped over one eye. She looked like a model, and her fingernails were so long she could have used them to spread peanut butter on bread.

"You were right, Luella," the woman was saying to Mrs. Willderby. "This place *is* a disaster. Good heavens, wherever did they get these lamps?" The two women laughed until they noticed me standing in the doorway.

"We like those lamps," I said. "We've had them for as long as I can remember. We like everything in here. We don't want it changed."

Mrs. Willderby patted me on the head. "Now, now, Natalie. Why don't you eat some breakfast so you won't be so grumpy."

"I'm not grumpy," I said. "I just don't like people barging in before I'm awake." I stomped into the kitchen. It took me about five minutes to find the cereal, because Frank had rearranged everything. Mom and I always left it on the kitchen table so it would be handy in the morning. We always left just about everything on the kitchen table, but Frank liked things neat. I was even grumpier by the time I got back into the living room.

Mom was sitting on the couch, dazed. Mrs. Willderby and the decorator had books of fabric samples spread out across the coffee table.

"I don't know," Mom said. "This is all so sudden, I haven't had a chance to think about it."

"Don't worry your head about it, my dear," the decorator said. "If you just leave everything to me, I'm sure I'll come up with a room you'll just love."

"Well, I think Anne should have some say in this," Frank said. "After all, she works in an art gallery. She's very artistic."

"Sometimes one is artistic but can't apply it to her own home," the decorator said, glancing around the room. "That's where I come in."

"I know you'll love Danielle's work," Mrs. Willderby said. "What you need is a really nice formal living room for entertaining."

Mom ran her fingers through her hair. "I don't do any entertaining. I just want a living room we can live in."

"Nonsense," Mrs. Willderby said. "When you're married to an important man, you need to entertain important people in your home. Now that Danielle has seen the room and taken the measurements, we'll be getting on our way." Mrs. Willderby and Danielle gathered up all their books of samples and left. Mom still sat on the couch, looking helplessly around the room.

"They can't do this," I said. "They can't just walk into our house and decide to change everything. Not if we don't want it changed."

Mom traced her fingers along the worn places in the arm of the couch. "Mother Willderby's doing us a favor, Natalie. We really should have a home that's more presentable. I'm sure we can come up with a room design we all like."

"What do you mean, 'presentable'?" I yelled. "Why is it that everything about us has to change?" I looked Frank right in the eye. "If you didn't like us the way we were, you shouldn't have married Mom in the first place. I'm sick of you," I said. "I'm sick of everything!"

I ran out the door, slamming it behind me. I needed to talk to Carla. I had run almost half a block before I remembered Carla was at *my* house, not hers.

I tried to sneak in the kitchen door, but Mom was there, making breakfast. "That was some exit," she said. "I hope you've calmed down. Did you forget Carla was here?"

"No, I didn't forget," I said, brushing past her. "I just needed some fresh air."

Carla was still asleep when I got upstairs. I closed my door and shook her shoulder. "Carla, wake up. It's an emergency."

Carla jumped out of bed, her eyes wide. "Okay,

stay calm," she said. She ran over to the door and started running her hands over it.

"What are you doing?" I asked.

"Don't you remember what that fireman said in school during Fire Safety Week? You never open a door if it feels hot. This one's fine. Let's get out of here." She grabbed my arm and yanked me through the door.

"Carla, there's no fire."

"What's the emergency, then?"

I pulled her back into the room and closed the door. "Frank's mother wants to get us all new furniture."

Carla stared at me for a few seconds, then climbed back into bed. "That," she said, pulling the covers up over her chin, "is *not* an emergency. Wake me up if the house catches on fire."

The weekend went by too fast. Mrs. Ackerman came over to pick Carla up Sunday night. "You're going to love the new house," she said, digging a picture out of her purse. "Your room is twice as big as the one you have now, and there's a park right behind us that you can see from your window."

Carla studied the picture. "Does it have a tree-house?"

"No, but I'm sure your father could build one just like he did here. There's a good-sized backyard with several trees."

Mom looked at the picture over Carla's shoulder. "It looks great. How soon will you be moving?"

"That's the best part," Mrs. Ackerman said. "Charlie's company found a mover that can take our things tomorrow afternoon."

"Tomorrow!" Mom said. "Can you be ready that soon?"

"I started packing the smaller things when Charlie first told us about the transfer," Mrs. Ackerman said. "When you've moved as often as we have, you don't have time to collect much junk. Carla, I think you'd better stay home tomorrow, so we can decide what you want to keep. The rest we'll give to the Salvation Army."

Carla handed the picture back to her mother and wrapped her arms around herself. "Okay, Mom. I guess we'd better get going."

"Do you want me to come over tonight and help?" I asked.

Carla shook her head. "I have to do it myself."

"I'll come over right after school tomorrow," I said.

I went back up to my room after Carla left. The house seemed empty, even though I could hear Mom and Frank talking downstairs. When Carla and I talked about her moving, it had seemed farther away. Now it was going to happen tomorrow. I felt numb.

I heard Mom's footsteps coming up the stairs, so I opened my door. "I can't believe Carla's moving tomorrow, Mom. I thought we'd have more time to get used to the idea."

"Mr. Ackerman's company wants them to make the move, so they're speeding things up, honey. It does seem awfully fast, though. I'd hate to clear out of here in a day."

"Can you come in and talk for a while, Mom?"

Mom looked at her watch. "I have to get to the supermarket before it closes. Frank and I are making crepes for supper and I'm out of eggs. Why don't you come along with me?"

"No, never mind," I said. I felt as if I would burst into tears any second, and I didn't want to be in public when it happened.

I stretched out on my bed and stared at the ceiling, watching it turn pink from the sunset. When I'd felt like this before, I could always call Carla. I could call her now, but she'd be busy packing. From now on, I could only call her every other Friday night after eleven. Suddenly I thought of calling Christa. We used to fight a lot when we were younger, but we'd been getting along pretty well for the past few years. I found her number in my desk drawer and dialed it.

"East tower, tenth floor," a voice said.

"Christa? Is that you?"

"Yes, who's this?"

"It's me, Natalie. I didn't know you had a phone right in your room."

"We don't, but it's just outside in the hall. Beth and I are usually the ones who answer it. So what's up at home?"

"Nothing. I just felt like talking to you. How do you like college?"

"It's better than I ever imagined," Christa said. "I'm suddenly an adult, you know? Nobody's nagging me to do my homework or go to bed on time."

"That sounds great. Are you getting along with your roommate?"

"Everybody thinks we're sisters. Beth and I even think alike."

"People think you're sisters?"

"Well, Beth is almost like a sister," Christa said, "only she doesn't bug me all the time like some sisters I could mention."

My throat tightened. I couldn't say anything for a minute.

"Nat? You still there?"

"Is that all you remember about me?" I asked, my voice wavering. "That I bugged you all the time?"

"Hey, take it easy. I was kidding. What's happened to your sense of humor?"

I started to cry. "Oh, Christa, everything is going wrong. Mom and Frank are acting like a couple of newlyweds."

"They *are* newlyweds," Christa said. "How are they supposed to act?"

"I don't know. It just seems weird being here with the two of them. And Frank's mother is butting in all the time. And . . . and the worst thing is, Carla's moving away—tomorrow!"

Christa's voice got soft. "I'm sorry, Nat. I know you and Carla are really close."

"She's the only friend I have, Christa. I don't know what I'm going to . . ."

Christa's voice cut in, shouting but muffled, as if she had her hand over the receiver. "Hey, wait up, you guys. I'll be right there." Then she sounded normal again. "Nat, I have to go. Everybody's heading for the dining hall."

"Okay," I mumbled. "I'm sorry I bothered you."

"You didn't bother me," Christa said. "Listen, I have an idea. Maybe later this year you could come down here and visit. You could stay in our room, and Beth and I will take you around to classes and stuff. What do you think?"

"That would be great, Christa."

"Hang in there, Nat. You'll make some new friends before you know it. And don't forget—you're still my favorite sister."

I sat there by the phone for a few minutes after I hung up. At least now I had something to look forward to. And maybe Christa was right. I could find new friends at school. With Carla around, I hadn't really made an effort. From now on, I'd have to try harder.

Chapter Ten

It seemed funny to walk to school alone the next morning. I'd done it before, when Carla was sick, but this was different. This was for good.

When I got to Kretzmer, the street right before the school, Sarah Birnbaum, one of the smartest kids in our class, turned onto the sidewalk just ahead of me. I didn't know her well, but Sarah had been in our class two years ago. This was my chance to make a new friend. After all, I was pretty smart, too, even if I didn't get all A's. I never really worked that hard on schoolwork, because Carla and I had so many other interesting things to do. I could get A-pluses if I put my mind to it.

"Hi," I said falling into step with Sarah. "Remember me? I'm Natalie Hanson."

She gave me a blank look. "Hi."

"What did you think of that math homework last night?" I asked. "Wasn't it just fascinating?"

Another blank look.

I wasn't about to give up. "Don't you just love numbers? I mean the way you can do so many things with them, like adding and subtracting and multiplying and dividing. You just keep coming up with all these fascinating answers." I was practically running to keep up with her. Sarah seemed to be trying to escape as we climbed the front steps to the school. "And what about those fractions? Aren't they just fascinating? I find the whole thing just . . . fascinating, don't you?"

"Yeah, sure, see you around." Sarah ducked into the classroom across from mine. Who wanted to be her friend? Sarah Birnbaum might be smart, but she sure couldn't hold up her end of a conversation.

Berna Jean turned around when I slipped into my seat. "Nice outfit, Natalie," she said, sending Mavis and Kimberly into a giggling fit.

I automatically looked over at Carla's desk for security. Of course, the desk was empty. I tried to block out Berna Jean and her friends for the rest of the morning.

Lunch was the worst part of the day. I spotted a table that just had two girls from my class. They were talking and laughing as I approached. "Hi," I said. "Mind if I sit here?"

"These two seats are saved," the redhead said. "You can sit at the other end of the table, though."

They went back to their talking and giggling, never

including me in their conversation. They had lowered their voices almost to a whisper. Carla and I used to do that at lunch when we had important things to talk about and someone sat at our table. Now I knew what it felt like to be an outsider.

School was finally over, and I ran all the way home. I stopped in the house just long enough to drop off my books, then took off for Carla's house. I wanted to have as much time as possible with her before the moving van got there.

When I got to the end of Carla's block, I saw the van was already in their driveway.

By the time I got to her house, the movers had taken out the living room furniture and loaded it into the truck. Mrs. Ackerman's car wasn't in the garage. I called in the front door, but there was no answer.

"They ain't here," one of the movers said. I couldn't believe I'd missed saying good-bye. I ran into the backyard and climbed up into the treehouse. From there, I could watch the parade of furniture coming out of the house. First there were the beds from upstairs. Carla's dresser was next, then the big wooden chest she used to store her stuffed animal collection. I couldn't help crying as I watched the last bits of Carla's family disappear. Pretty soon there would be strangers living in her house.

Suddenly I felt the treehouse move. "What are you doing up here?" Carla asked, climbing through the opening in the floor.

I jumped to my feet. "When I didn't see the car, I thought you'd gone."

"We just took a load of stuff down to the Salvation Army. We stopped at your house on the way home, but nobody was there." Carla sat in the corner and pulled her knees close to her chest. "We're leaving in a few minutes, though."

"It's happening too fast," I said. "I'm not ready for this."

"Nobody's ever ready for this," Carla said.

"Carla! Where are you? We have to get going," Mrs. Ackerman called.

"Coming, Mom," Carla called back. She got up and grabbed the treasue box. "You want to keep this stuff?"

"It's more than half yours. We could sort through it."

"There's no time." She shoved the box into my hands. "You can use the treehouse until the house is sold. Nobody's going to mind."

"Okay," I said, putting the box back in its place.

Mrs. Ackerman was waiting for us in the driveway. "Oh, Natalie, I'm glad you came over. We were afraid we wouldn't get to say good-bye to you." She gave me a big hug and kissed me on the top of the head. "I'm going to miss you, kiddo. When you come out to visit us, I'll make you stew with dumplings and take you to an Indians game."

"Great," I said, barely able to talk over the lump in my throat.

"Well, this is it, kids," Mrs. Ackerman said. She took one last long look and got into the car.

Carla and I hugged until we both started to cry. "I was right," Carla said. "It's much easier to cut off a friendship before you move. This way hurts too much."

She jumped into the car and they took off, with Mrs. Ackerman honking the horn. I stood there waving until they disappeared around a corner.

I wasn't ready to go home yet, so I climbed back into the treehouse. I huddled in the corner and let the tears come. There was an ache in the middle of my chest, where my heart should be.

I pulled the treasure box closer and looked inside. There were all our bottles of colored nail polish. I'd never have the guts to wear rainbow nails in school without Carla.

When I stopped crying, I took the treasure box and headed home. Mom put her arm around me as I came into the kitchen. "So, Carla's gone, huh? I saw the moving van."

I couldn't talk. I just bit my lip and nodded.

"I don't suppose you'd believe me if I told you, but you will make new friends."

"Not like Carla, Mom," I said, putting my hand on my chest. "If you hurt right here, is that what they mean by heartache?"

Mom brushed the hair out of my eyes. "I think it's

exactly what they mean. I have some news that may make you feel better, though. How would you like to spend next week with your father?"

"Really? How come?" Christa and I always spent a month with Dad each summer, but we'd already done that in June.

Mom pulled a brochure out of her purse. "I know it's sudden, but Frank's been saving this as a surprise. He's taking me to the Caribbean. Look, isn't this beautiful?" There were pictures of blue water and white sand and people in bathing suits, laughing. I tried to picture Frank as one of those people, but I couldn't. He'd probably wear a white shirt and tie with his swimming trunks.

"What about school, Mom?" Dad lived in Syracuse, about an hour and a half away. There was no way he could get me back and forth to school every day.

"Did you forget?" Mom asked. "It's teachers' conference week. You have the first two days off, so you'll only be missing school Wednesday through Friday. I'm sure you'll be able to make up the work."

"You're right, I forgot. When is Dad coming to get me?"

"He'll pick you up here Sunday night. Frank and I have to leave by five-thirty, and your father can't get here much before six, so you may have to be here alone for a short time."

"No problem. I can stay alone."

Mom smiled. "I don't know what your father has planned, but I'm sure you'll have a great week."

"Yeah, I always do. I love doing stuff with Dad." This would be the first time I'd have Dad all to myself, without Christa. Things were beginning to look up.

Just then Frank came into the room. "Did I hear you say Natalie will be waiting here by herself? I don't think that's a good idea. I'll ask my mother to come over and baby-sit."

"Baby-sit!" I yelled. "Baby-sitters are for little kids."

"Natalie," Frank said. "You're only eleven years old. That's not exactly an adult."

"But I've been on my own lots of times. Why do you treat me like a baby?" I ran up to my room and slammed the door. I heard Mom's footsteps on the stairs and braced myself for another fight. I hated the arguments Mom and I had been having lately, mostly about the way Frank and his mother were taking over our lives. It wasn't fair. Mom was the one who decided to marry Frank, not me.

I threw the clothes from my bed onto the floor and stretched out. My life was turning into such a mess. I'd have one great week with Dad, but then I'd be back here again, and nothing would have changed.

Mom knocked on the door.

"Come in," I mumbled, rolling over to face the wall. I could feel her sitting down on my bed.

"Natalie, what's happening to you? You never used to act like this."

"I never had to live with Frank before."

"Do you resent the fact that Frank and I are taking a trip together?"

Her voice sounded as if she were about to cry, so I rolled over to see her face. She had tears spilling over, but she wiped them away quickly.

"I don't care about you and Frank going away," I said. "I just don't want to be stuck here with Mrs. Willderby."

"But it would only be for a short time," Mom said. "No more than half an hour. That wouldn't be so bad, would it?"

"Mom, in a half hour. Mrs. Willderby could have this whole house torn down and rebuilt. You really want to let her loose in here?"

Mom smiled. "Mother Willderby *is* a bit much, isn't she? Okay, you've made your point, Nat. I'll convince Frank you can wait here alone."

The phone was ringing when I got home from school the next day. I fumbled with my key and got inside to grab it before it stopped. It was Dad. "Thank heaven you're there," he said. "I was just about to hang up."

"Mom and Frank aren't home from work yet," I said, dumping my books on the kitchen table. "Mom told me I'm spending next week with you."

"Well, pumpkin, that was the plan, but I'm afraid things aren't going to work out."

I sat down, gripping the receiver. "Why not?"

"I have to make a business trip to Japan. Charlie Baxter was supposed to go, but he's having emergency gallbladder surgery today. I'm next in line, so I get stuck. I wanted to talk to your mother about it. I have to leave right away—barely have time to stuff things into my suitcase."

I tried to hold back the tears. Now I didn't even have the week with Dad to look forward to.

"I'm really sorry, pumpkin," Dad said, pausing just long enough to realize I wasn't saying anything. "I thought maybe you could go spend the week with your grandmother. I just tried to call her, but her line is busy."

"Grandma talks on the phone for hours," I said. "You'll never get her."

The last thing I needed right now was a trip to Grandma's. She treated me more like a baby than Frank did. She'd barely let me out of her sight in the retirement trailer park where she lived. There weren't any other kids around, and the only thing to do was play shuffleboard.

If only I had a life of my own, like Christa. Nobody made decisions for college students. They could do anything they wanted to. Suddenly a plan started to form in my mind. Maybe I wouldn't have to go to Grandma's after all. Maybe I could go someplace terrific instead, and nobody would know.

"I don't know what to do," Dad said. "I don't want

to leave before I know everything's all set for you. I really need to talk to your mother. Do you have any idea when she'll be back? I could call again from the airport."

"She's . . . uh . . . not coming home for quite a while," I said, knowing Mom might pull into the driveway any second.

"Well, this is a real mess," Dad said. "I'd tell the company to send someone else, but they don't take kindly to that. There have been a lot of layoffs lately, and I can't afford to be in the next batch to get fired. I'm really in a bind here."

I pulled aside the curtain to look down the street. Mom's car was just coming around the corner. "Look, Dad, you're going to miss your plane. I'll tell Mom what's happened, and she can call Grandma. I'm sure it'll be okay. Grandma never goes anywhere."

"I can't believe you're taking this so well, Nat. Sometimes I forget how grown-up you've become. I'll call you as soon as I get back. If I get home before the end of the week, I'll come pick you up at Grandma's."

"Oh no! You can't do that!"

"Why not?"

"Because . . . because it would really hurt Grandma's feelings. You know she loves to have her grandchildren come visit. Don't worry about anything, Dad. Go catch your plane. I'll tell Mom what's happened, and she'll take care of everything."

"Well . . . it's against my better judgment, but I guess we don't have any other choice. Tell your mother I'm sorry about this."

"I will, Dad. Now hurry up or you'll miss your plane."

I hung up the exact instant Mom came through the door.

Mom dumped two bags of groceries on the table. "What's up? Somebody call?"

"I was just going to call Carla," I said, "then I remembered she was gone."

Mom gave me a big hug. "Old habits die hard, don't they? Any luck finding new friends at school?"

I opened a cereal box from one of the bags and grabbed a handful. "Everything's going great," I lied. "I met some new kids today."

"Didn't I tell you you'd make new friends? You probably overlooked some terrific kids because you were always tied up with Carla. I'm sure before long you'll have more friends than you know what to do with."

"You're right, Mom. I may be voted Miss Popularity any day now." Mom missed the sarcasm in my voice because Frank came in, and she started to give him a big welcome home kiss. That was fine. I had to start working on my plan.

I slipped out quietly and went up to Christa's room. There was something I had to find. I just hoped

Christa hadn't taken it to school with her. When I opened the second drawer of her desk, I found it sitting on top—the bus schedule to Corinthia. She'd used it when she'd gone to orientation this summer.

I sat down at Christa's desk and turned on the light. Then I slipped a pen and a clean piece of paper out of the top drawer and began writing out my plan, only this time I wasn't going to leave it on the kitchen table. I just wanted to write it all down so I could get everything straight in my mind.

Frank was right. It really paid to plan ahead.

Chapter Eleven

Frank paced back and forth across the living room, checking his watch. "I just don't feel right about leaving Natalie here alone. What if her father has car trouble and doesn't make it?"

"Look," Mom said, "in spite of his other faults, Bill is very responsible when it comes to Natalie. He'd rent a car if he had to. He promised he'd be here, and he will. I guarantee it."

"I still wish you'd let me call Mother. I'm sure she'd be more than happy to come over."

I caught Mom's eye, and she winked at me. "We've been all over this, Frank," Mom said. "Nat's going to be fine. Make sure you don't lose the phone number I gave you, Natalie. That's just in case you have to reach us in an emergency."

"I have it, Mom."

Frank took out his wallet and handed me twenty dollars. "Here, Natalie, use this for some extra spending money."

"You don't need to do that, Frank," Mom said. "Bill will get her anything she needs."

"I know I don't have to. I'd like to."

"Thanks, Frank," I said, slipping the money into my wallet. Grandma had sent me twenty dollars for a birthday present, and I had planned to use that for the cab and bus. Now I wouldn't have to. I had five dollars left over from my allowance. I should have plenty.

Frank looked at his watch again. "All right. If we don't leave now, we might miss the plane."

Mom hugged me. "Well, here we go. Have a great week with your father, honey. We'll see you next Sunday night."

I called a cab as soon as they left, and it got me to the bus station in plenty of time. My plan had worked out perfectly. Mom and Frank thought I was with Dad, and Dad thought I was with Grandma. Grandma didn't know about Mom and Frank's trip, so she thought I was home—if she thought about me at all. If she called, she'd assume we were all out. Besides, Mom was the one who usually made the calls, because Grandma didn't like to spend money on long distance. And now I was off to Corinthia. Wait till the Innies heard about that. I'd be the only kid in the whole class who had ever gone to college!

I got on the bus and found a seat toward the rear next to a window. I leaned back and watched as we left the city. The bus took longer than driving in the car. It stopped in a couple of small towns along the way.

Pretty soon the road was following the lake, and I knew we were getting close to Corinthia. It wasn't long before we pulled into a station.

"This station stop is Corinthia," the driver announced. I looked out the window. There were a few dingy, beat-up buildings, nothing like what I'd seen on campus. Where were the fountains and the towers? I stopped when I got to the driver's seat. "Excuse me, but where's the college?"

"This bus just goes to the town of Corinthia. The campus is on top of the hill," he said. "That cab over there can take you up."

I got off the bus and looked around. I could see the lights from the towers way up on the hill, but it was much too far to walk, especially at night. I checked my wallet. Only two dollars and thirty-five cents left. There was a bright yellow cab waiting by the curb. "How much does it cost to go to the Corinthia campus?" I asked.

The cab driver yawned. "Four dollars. You goin' up there?"

"Uh . . . no thanks." I said. I went back into the station and found a phone. I dialed Christa's number. It rang for a long time. What if she wasn't here? What if she'd gone out somewhere and wasn't getting back until late? I'd be stuck in this creepy bus station. It was dark out now. Just as I was about to hang up, a girl's voice answered. "Tenth floor, East Tower."

"Christa?" I asked. "Is that you?"

"No, wait a minute. I'll see if she's here."

The girl must have dropped the phone because the receiver kept clunking against the wall, boinging in my ear. It seemed to take forever before Christa got on the line. "Hello," she said.

"Christa, it's me, Natalie. Boy, am I glad to hear your voice."

"Hi, Nat. How are you? What's going on at home?"

"I don't know. I'm not there. I'm here."

"Here in Corinthia? I didn't know you guys were coming down to visit."

"It's just me," I said. "I'm alone at the bus station."

"Natalie, you didn't do something stupid like run away from home, did you? Because if you did, you're going to go right back. I'm not getting in trouble with Mom and Frank."

I had to think fast. "What do you mean? Didn't you get Mom's letter?"

"What letter?"

"The one about her and Frank going on a trip and me coming to stay with you?"

"No. I didn't get any letter. Why didn't Mom call me?"

"She tried, but she couldn't get you. The trip was real sudden. She sent you a special delivery letter."

"I don't believe a word of this," Christa said. "Even Mom isn't that disorganized."

"Okay," I said. "I ran away—just for a week. Mom and Frank are on a trip. They're coming back next Sunday." I explained how I fixed it so everybody thought I was with somebody else. "Please don't be mad, Christa."

"Mad? I could wring your little neck." There was a brief silence at the other end of the line. "All right. Go out of the bus station and get a cab to my dorm. You know where my room is."

"I can't," I said. "I don't have enough money."

Christa sighed. "I'll be waiting for you outside, and I'll pay for the taxi."

I hung up and went over to the cab. "I'd like to go up to the Corinthia College campus."

The driver got out and put my suitcase in the front seat while I climbed in back. Then he jumped into the driver's seat and took off, all in one motion. It felt like a rocket launch, only we were going horizontally instead of vertically. He hung a U-turn that skidded me to the opposite side of the slippery plastic-covered seat.

"I'm not in any hurry," I said when I could catch my breath. Either he didn't hear me or he didn't care. We barreled through the center of town and started up the hill.

I tried to think of something else, to keep myself from being scared to death. I hadn't counted on Christa being mad that I was here, but that didn't matter. Once I explained to her about what had been

going on at home, she'd understand. After all, Christa
knew what a pain Frank could be. And when I reminded her about Carla moving away and told her
about Mrs. Willderby and how I didn't have any
friends, she'd see why I had to get out of there.

The cab driver looked over his shoulder. "Which
dorm you going to?" he asked.

I told him East Tower, and he lurched up the final
hill, slamming to a stop right in front of Christa. She
paid him while I pulled my suitcase out of the front
seat.

The cab shot out of sight, and Christa and I stood
there facing each other.

"Why didn't you call ahead and tell me you were
coming?" she asked.

"I was afraid you'd talk me out of it."

"You're right. I would have."

"But you said on the phone that I could come and
visit you sometime."

"That didn't mean you could just come any time you
felt like it, Nat. This is a terrible week. Last week
would have been good, or even next week, but this
week is murder. I have a huge paper due."

"You don't have to entertain me," I said. "I'll just go
my own way and see what college life is like."

Christa stood with her arms folded, staring at me. It
was the same look I got from Mom when she got mad.
I started to cry.

"Oh, Nat, don't do that. It really is good to see you. I've missed you, even if you are a major pain sometimes." She gave me a quick hug. "We might as well make the best of this. Let's go up to the room."

"You're not going to tell Mom and Frank, are you?" I asked.

Christa bit her lip, then shrugged. "I guess not, as long as everything goes all right."

"You promise?"

Christa smiled. "Yes, I promise."

I felt happy for the first time in weeks. "Everything's going to be great. You'll see. Thanks, Christa."

"Sure. What are sisters for?"

The elevator was waiting for us. Christa pushed the button for ten, but it stopped at the fifth floor. Two guys in gym shorts jumped on, carrying water-filled balloons.

"Wait a minute, guys," Christa said. "If this is a floor war, let us off on ten before the attack, okay?"

Before they could say anything, the door opened again on seven, and we were bombarded with water balloons from the hall. The two guys in shorts ran out, slinging water balloons at their attackers. Christa pushed the close-door button, and we were safe. "Idiots," she mumbled, wiping the wet hair from her eyes. "Whoever coined the phrase 'college men' never visited this campus. There's not one male with a maturity level of more than twelve. Except Xandy, of course. He's different."

"Who?"

Christa smiled. "I guess you'd call him my boy-friend. His name is pronounced 'Zandy,' but it's spelled with an X. It's short for Alexander. Anyway, he's really nice—funny, too."

We got off on the tenth floor, which was just as noisy as it had been the day we brought Christa to college. Stereos were blasting four different songs.

"How do you sleep through this?" I asked.

"You get used to it. I don't even hear it anymore."

Christa opened the door to her room. There were little paths to the beds and desks, but otherwise it looked the same as the day we dropped her off. The whole room was piled almost knee-high with clothes and junk.

"Hi," Beth said, looking up from an art project she was working on. "It's good to see you again, Natalie. Christa says you're staying with us. We'll clear a spot for you." She grabbed a sleeping bag from the corner. "You can use this. I sleep in it when my bed's messed up, but I cleaned this morning."

Christa laughed. " 'Cleaned' means Beth dumped the junk from her bed onto the floor."

Beth piled some cartons up against the wall to make a space. "Hey, whatever works. Right, Natalie?" She tested out the cleared spot by rolling out her sleeping bag. "There. Perfect! We'll leave it rolled up until you're ready to go to bed."

Christa tossed my suitcase up onto her bunk. "You had supper at home, didn't you?"

"Not exactly," I said. All I'd had to eat was a package of cheese and peanut butter crackers from the machine in the bus station.

Christa dug around in her purse. "Here." She tossed me a package of cheese and peanut butter crackers, the same brand I'd eaten. "I was going to eat these while I studied, but you can have them. There's no place on campus to get food at this hour, unless we order pizza, and the cab almost cleaned me out of money."

"I'd help you out," Beth said, "but I'm broke."

Christa laughed. "You're always broke."

"It's the art supplies," Beth said. "They're so expensive. This piece of paper cost seven-fifty."

"Seven dollars and fifty cents for one piece of paper?" I asked.

Beth nodded. "It has a special finish so it takes the ink without spreading. When you put this much time into a project, you might as well use good materials."

I peeked over her shoulder. Beth was lettering a poem about the sea, and the letters formed the shape of a series of waves. "Wow, did you letter that by hand? I thought it was done on a printing press."

Beth laughed. "Don't I wish! I worked on this thing

all last week. We had to make a block of text fit into an unusual shape."

"You're probably tired, aren't you, Nat?" Christa asked. "When you want to get ready for bed, the bathroom's down at the end of the hall. You may have to wait in line. There's only one john on this floor, and fifteen girls use it."

I pulled out my pajamas and my toothbrush. "Fifteen people in one bathroom?"

Beth shrugged. "You get used to it. It's not so bad."

I finished off the crackers and headed down the hall. By the time I waited my turn and got back to the room, it was after ten o'clock. I wanted to stay up and soak up the college atmosphere, but I was so tired, I could hardly keep my eyes from closing.

"Well, good night," I said, rolling out Beth's sleeping bag.

Christa looked up from her computer. " 'Night, Nat. The music won't bother you, will it? Beth and I are used to having it on while we work."

"No, it's great. Frank makes me turn my radio off by eight o'clock every school night."

Christa's fingers paused on the keyboard. "That bad, huh? Can't say it surprises me."

"That's nothing," I said, dying to tell her what I'd been going through at home. "Wait till you hear about some of the other stuff he's done. Wait till I tell you about . . ."

Christa rubbed her forehead. "Look, Nat. I really want to hear about Frank, but not tonight, okay? I'm not even halfway through writing this paper. After I hand it in Tuesday morning, I'm all yours."

"You won't see much of me until Tuesday, either," Beth said. "That's when this calligraphy project is due—if I can get it finished by then. I should have chosen something simpler."

"You should have done it on my computer," Christa said. "I could have set that whole thing up for you in fifteen minutes."

Beth groaned. "I don't really want to hear that, Christa. Anyway, the art department would never approve. We're supposed to be developing our skills."

"The art department is still living in the Middle Ages. Watch this." Christa pushed a few keys, and the page she was working on molded itself into the shape of a star on the screen. "Or this." She drew something quickly with the mouse, and the letters formed a Christmas tree.

"You're making me crazy, you know," Beth said, bending closer over her paper as she carefully formed another letter.

I slipped into Beth's sleeping bag and listened to the two of them banter back and forth about computers. Beth's tape deck played some rock band in the background. The room was a mess, and nobody was yelling at them to clean it up. I crossed my arms behind my head to make a pillow, taking in all the posters on the walls. I was actually at college. I felt grownup, and I didn't have Frank and Mom nagging at me every two seconds. This was heaven, and I hadn't even had to wait seven years to get here!

Chapter Twelve

I was having a dream about a party. All around me I could hear people talking, and I could smell food—especially pizza. My feet felt weird, as if they were being weighted down with something. I rolled over and opened my eyes. The room was bright with light.

"Hey, Sleeping Beauty's awake," a male voice said. "Want something to eat?"

I rubbed my eyes and sat up. A skinny guy with glasses was sitting on the bottom of my sleeping bag.

"Hi," he said. "I wasn't crushing your feet, was I? There aren't too many places to sit in this room."

"Look who's talking," Beth said. "There aren't *any* places to sit in Xandy's room, which is why he always comes up here to bug us."

Xandy opened a bucket of chicken wings and held them out to me. "Did I or did I not supply the snacks for this study break? Help yourself."

I rubbed my eyes. "Study break? What time is it?"

Xandy looked at his watch. "Two-thirty."

"You mean two-thirty A.M.?"

Xandy grinned. "If it's P.M., I'm real late for my psych class."

I reached for a wing. "You mean you can have a party in the middle of the night and nobody yells at you?"

"Sure," Xandy said, "within reason, of course." He took three wings out of the bucket, and suddenly—I couldn't believe my eyes—he started juggling with them.

"Xandy, knock it off!" Christa said. "You're going to drop them."

"These wings were made for flying," Xandy said. "Besides, have I ever dropped anything when I juggled?"

"You don't really want an answer, do you?" Beth asked. "I know why he does that—so he can take three chicken wings at a time instead of just one."

I watched, fascinated, as the wings arched through the air, their red sauce glistening in the overhead light. Every two or three throws, Xandy would lick his fingers without missing a beat. Then he caught one in each hand, one in his mouth and took a bow.

I was the only one who clapped.

Xandy put the wings on a napkin and started to eat. "I'm glad there's someone in this room with good taste," he said. "Your sister and her roommate don't appreciate me. You want to see me juggle pizza?"

"No!" Christa and Beth shouted in unison. Xandy shrugged, then settled in to finish his wings and eat a couple of pieces of pizza.

Christa and Beth each ate a slice. Then Christa went back to her desk. "This has been great, Xandy, but if I don't get to work, I may flunk out by the end of the semester."

Xandy stood up. "Say no more. I'm off." He picked up the half-empty pizza box. "Anybody want another piece?" I was tempted to say yes, but I'd already had four wings and two slices of pizza. "Okay," Xandy said. "The guys on my floor will polish this off in no time." He winked at me and left.

It got pretty boring after that, with Beth and Christa both working, so I slipped back into my sleeping bag.

The next time I woke up, light was coming though the window. I sat up and looked around. Both bunk beds were empty.

Somebody laughed in the hall, and the door opened. "Oh, good, you're up," Christa said. "Here's something to eat." She handed me a jelly doughnut wrapped in a napkin.

"You went to breakfast without me?"

"I had to, Nat. The only way you can get into a dining room is with a student ID card."

"Couldn't you sneak me in?"

"No. There's always someone at the desk right as you go in. They run your card through the computer. That's how they keep track of how many meals you have each week."

Beth came in behind Christa. She was wearing a bathrobe, and her hair was still wet from the shower. "Too bad Natalie can't use my card. I hardly ever get the meals from the dining hall."

"Could I?" I asked, finishing the last of the doughnut. "I'm still hungry."

Christa dug through a pile of books on her desk and pulled out a thick notebook. "They're picture IDs. They'd never take you for Beth."

"It might work," Beth said. "My picture's out of focus. It doesn't even look like me." She held up the small plastic card. In her picture, her hair was pulled up into a ponytail on one side, and she was wearing a lot of makeup. I thought I could probably look like that with the same hairdo and a little eye shadow. "I keep my ID in here, if you want to use it." Beth slipped the card into the top drawer of her desk.

"Forget it," Christa said. "It could get us all in trouble." She looked at her watch. "Darn! I'm going to be late for my eight o'clock. Allison is a real stickler for punctuality."

"Who's Allison?" I asked.

"My professor for broadcast production."

"You call your teachers by their first names?"

"This is college, Nat. It's not like your teacher in fifth grade. We're all adults here."

College was even better than I'd imagined. I couldn't picture calling Miss Simkewicz "Geraldine."

"Can I go with you to class?" I asked.

"You're not even dressed."

"I can throw something on real quick. Please? I want to see what your classes are like."

"This class is in a TV studio, Natalie. I'm afraid you'd be in the way."

"Let her go with you," Beth said. "I'm leaving for the art studio, and she'd be here all alone."

Christa sighed. "Okay, but make it snappy. And put something warm on. It's cold out this morning."

Christa opened her dresser drawer and pulled out a white sweat shirt with Corinthia written across the front in green. "You do have something warm, don't you?"

"Not exactly," I said, slipping into the jeans and T-shirt from the day before. "It was hot at home when I left."

"Here, then, wear this." Christa tossed me the sweat shirt and pulled out a blue one for herself. I slipped mine over my head and stood in front of the mirror. With the Corinthia emblem across my chest, I looked like a real college student.

"Come on, Nat. Never mind what you look like. I

have to get to class in time to ask Allison's permission
for you to be there. If she says no, you'll have to come
back to the room."

I jammed my feet into my sneakers without both-
ering to tie them and took off after Christa. We ran
across the green in front of the dorm and down some
cement stairs. That's when I tripped on a shoelace and
dove headfirst down the last three steps.

Christa spun around. "Nat! Are you hurt?"

A small group of students started to gather around
us, then moved on when Christa waved them away. I
bit my lip to hold back the tears. I had ripped a hole
in the elbow of Christa's sweat shirt, and a red stain of
blood was oozing out around my mangled elbow. "It's
okay," I mumbled. "Just a little scrape."

"Little? You're bleeding all over my new sweat
shirt."

"Well, excuse me," I said. "Usually I try not to
bleed, but I forgot this time."

Christa helped me up. "I'm sorry. Here, use this."
She dug in her purse and pulled out a tissue. "We
really have to hurry. We're doing newscasts this week,
and the whole thing is timed. If I throw it off, it will
lower the student director's grade. Tie your shoelaces,
will you?"

I could feel my raw skin stinging as it rubbed against
the ragged edges of the sweat shirt. I jerked a quick
knot in each shoe, and we took off again. We cut

through the student union—in one door and out the other end. There were lots of students milling around, but by the time we got to the Communications Building, there were only a few stragglers running late to class like us.

We went down the hall and through a set of tall double doors. Inside, there was just a tiny room with another set of double doors straight ahead. Christa pointed to a red sign that read "On Air." "We're lucky that sign isn't lit."

"Why?"

"Because that would mean they'd already started taping and we couldn't get in." We went through a second set of doors into a long room that had lights hanging from a grid overhead. Heavy curtains hung from three of the walls—one light gray, one black, and one bright blue. Three kids wearing headsets were standing behind TV cameras, moving them into position.

"Where the heck were you, Christa?" one girl said. "You're talent today—weather."

"What did she mean?" I said, as Christa shoved me across the room, dodging cameras.

"I have to do the weather report. I wish I'd had a chance to look at the maps ahead of time. I'll just have to wing it."

"How do you know what the weather's going to be?"

"I don't. I read it off the TelePrompTer on the camera."

We went into the control room, and Christa introduced me to Allison, who was wearing jeans and looked about two years older than Christa.

"You can sit on that stool in the corner," Allison said. "You'll have to stay out of the way, but you should be able to see pretty well from here."

"This is Jake," Christa said, pointing to the guy who was sitting next to Allison. "He's the director today."

Jake looked over his shoulder. "Get out there, Christa. You're weather."

"I know! I know!" She slipped out of the control room, giving me a little wave.

I settled back into my seat and looked around. There was lots of important-looking equipment, a long board filled with switches, and two TV monitors up above. Several other students were sitting at the equipment table, some wearing earphones.

Jake started giving commands, and images appeared on the monitors.

It was weird watching a newscast from behind the scenes. Jake gave another series of commands. "Ready take . . . ready dissolve . . . ready fade up camera one . . . ready theme . . . ready announce."

The girl sitting next to him kept turning on switches. Each one glowed as she hit it. Then Jake started counting. "In ten, nine, eight, seven, six, five, four, three, . . . dissolve camera one . . . ready take chromakey."

The theme for the news show came up with the logo, and I could see two people at a news desk, just like on TV at home. After a few news stories there was a pause while they ran some commercials; then the anchorwoman said, "And now with today's weather, here's Christa Hanson."

I craned my neck to see Christa in the studio, but she wasn't at the desk. All of a sudden, Jake groaned. "Oh, great. Her shirt dropped out."

"Her shirt dropped off?" I said, jumping up from my stool. I couldn't believe my sister was going topless on TV. If Mom heard about this, she'd kill her.

I looked at the monitor and there was Christa—at least part of her—in front of the weather map. Her head was floating over Lake Huron, and her hands were flapping around the Midwest like confused birds, but the rest of her was missing. It looked like one of those magic acts where someone is sawed in half.

I jumped out of my seat and went over by the long board of switches. I leaned over the board until I could see Christa through the glass. She was standing in front of a blue curtain and her whole body was there.

I looked back at the monitor. Christa kept going with her weather forecast, but her face was bright red, which stood out against a green thunderstorm over New England. She pointed out a warm front, and her hand zipped out to the West Coast like a 747. I started laughing, and that's when I lost my balance a little and leaned on the board of switches.

"Hey," Jake said, "what happened? We went to black."

Both TV screens had gone blank. I noticed there was a switch under my hand and it was glowing.

"Geez," someone at the table said, "the kid hit the downstream keyer."

I didn't know what that meant, but I was pretty sure it wasn't good.

Chapter Thirteen

"I don't even know what I did," I said, running to keep up with Christa.

"It's what you didn't do—like staying where you were told."

"I did, until they said your shirt dropped off."

"Dropped *out*, not off," Christa corrected. "I made a complete idiot of myself. I was wearing the same blue as the curtain. The chromakey makes anything that color on screen disappear, and the weather map replaces it."

"I don't understand." I ducked around a couple of kids who were coming out of Christa's dorm. "Besides, the fact you wore blue wasn't my fault. And I didn't mean to hit that switch."

"I know you didn't do it on purpose, Natalie, but just having you here is throwing me all off schedule. If we hadn't been late for class, I would have remembered I was going to do the weather this morning and I wouldn't have worn the blue shirt."

"I won't cause any problems in the next class," I said.

Christa stopped in front of the elevator. "You're right about that, because you aren't going to the next class. Go on up to the room. I'll bring you something back from lunch later."

I looked at my watch. "But it's only nine o'clock. Lunch is three hours away."

"Look, you can watch Beth's TV or play my tapes. That should make time pass."

Before I could say anything else, she shoved the key into my hand and took off.

I pushed the button for the elevator and went up to the tenth floor. The dorm was pretty quiet. I figured everybody must be in class. I switched on the TV and watched a couple of game shows, but it wasn't much fun to guess the answers by myself. Carla and I used to play Jeopardy together all the time. We got a lot of the answers right, too, even the Daily Doubles.

I wondered how Carla was doing in her new school. I hadn't written to her yet because I hadn't had anything to tell her until now. I sat down at the desk and tore a blank sheet of paper out of Christa's notebook. I wrote about everything that had happened since Carla had left, except for the part about me goofing up in the TV class. I found an envelope in Christa's desk drawer and wrote Carla's name on the front. That's when I realized I didn't have her new address. We'd both been so upset when she left, neither of us had thought of it. Not only that, Carla would be calling me on Friday, but I wouldn't be home.

That's when I had a brilliant idea. I wrote her old address on the envelope and added the words "Please Forward."

My stomach started to grumble, and I looked at the clock. It was only quarter after eleven. If Christa didn't go to lunch until noon, it could be close to one before she brought something back to me. A person could starve to death by then.

Maybe I could go to the dining hall by myself and pretend to be Beth. After all, she had said I could use her ID. I pulled the card out of her desk and studied it. I looked at my reflection in the mirror. I experimented with pulling my hair up in a one-sided ponytail. When I squinted my eyes, I looked a little bit like Beth's picture. Then I dug into the makeup box on Christa's dresser and started my transformation.

It took quite a while, but I finally finished. If I didn't look like Beth, at least I looked a lot older than twelve. There was just one thing missing—well, two things. I put on one of Christa's bras and stuffed it with Kleenex until I had just the right effect. Then I rolled up the sleeve of Christa's sweat shirt to cover up the bloody ripped part, put a Band-Aid on my elbow, and slipped Beth's ID into my jeans pocket.

"Okay, Beth," I said to my reflection in the mirror, "let's go to lunch."

*   *   *

I noticed I was getting quite a few admiring looks as I walked across campus. When I reached the dining hall, I got in line behind a bunch of guys who were having an argument about some baseball player's batting average. I watched how they handed their cards to the lady at the desk. When it was my turn, I gave her Beth's card and tried to act as if I did this every day, three times a day. She didn't even look at me. I couldn't believe it. My disguise had worked.

I was so hungry when I went through the cafeteria line, I loaded up on everything I could get my hands on. Then I looked around for Christa, but I didn't see her. I found a table over on one side of the dining hall and set down my tray. I had enough food for three meals. I looked around at the people at the other tables. I felt like a real college student. I finally belonged somewhere. If only I could stay here for good.

I concentrated on my food at first. Then I noticed three girls at the next table who sort of reminded me of the Innies. They seemed to be watching me, so I smiled and gave them a little wave. Suddenly, they all burst out laughing. Then one of them said something to the others, and they all laughed again. I could feel my face turning red.

This wasn't any different from being in school at home. There were still Innies and Outies, and as usual I was the Outie. My lunch didn't taste so great anymore. I got up, and there was another wave of laughter from the table next to me. I felt as if everybody was watching me. I was heading for the exit when I crashed into somebody.

"Hey, slow down," he said.

"Sorry," I mumbled. The whole room looked blurry through my tears.

I kept walking toward the door, but he caught my arm. "Wait, Natalie. I thought that was you sitting at the table alone. What's the matter?" It was Xandy.

"I shouldn't have come here," I said. "I'll go back to the room and wait for Christa."

"She's going through the cafeteria line. As long as you're here, why don't you come over and sit with us?"

He led me back to my table and picked up my tray. "You left most of your food."

"I lost my appetite. Besides, Christa's going to be mad about me sneaking in here."

"I was going to ask you about that. Come on. We're sitting over by the window. How did you get in here, anyway?"

I followed him and sat in the chair he pulled out for me. "I used Beth's ID. She told me I could."

"I see." Xandy sat across from me. "That would explain the . . . war paint."

"I'm not very good at makeup," I said. "Did I overdo it?"

Xandy nodded. "Let's just say it's a little extreme. Why don't you run into the john and wash it off before Christa sees you."

"Good idea," I said. "Don't go away. I'll be right back."

"While you're in there, why don't you get rid of some of the . . . you know." He pointed to his chest.

"Oh, okay," I said. "I guess I overdid that, too."

Xandy nodded. "Just a tad."

By the time I got back to the table, I was my old boring self again. It was a good thing because Christa was there, too.

"Hi," I said, slipping into my chair.

Christa glared at me. "I can't believe you came over here and snuck in with Beth's ID. Didn't I tell you I'd bring you something back from lunch?"

"I know, Christa, but I got so sick of sitting in the room. And I was getting hungry. I didn't think you'd mind. Besides, Beth said I could, remember?"

Christa sighed. "Okay. I'm sorry, Nat. What happened this morning wasn't really your fault. I guess I've been a little hard on you."

"Does that mean I can go to classes with you this afternoon?" I asked.

Christa opened a small packet of ketchup and squeezed it over her hamburger. "I have a lecture class after lunch. What's one extra body in a class of eighty-five? But I don't want you sneaking into meals anymore. If they catch you using Beth's ID, you can get us all in trouble."

At least I wasn't going to be stuck in the room all day. I had a feeling Xandy had talked to Christa about me while I was cleaning up. I liked Xandy, and he seemed to like me.

After lunch, we went back to the room to get Christa's books, then headed out for her afternoon class. It was in a huge room with the floor slanted down to the front like a movie theater. The room was packed with kids, but we found two seats together toward the back.

The professor stood down in front and droned on and on about stuff I couldn't even understand. Christa was scribbling notes furiously in her notebook. I didn't know how she could stay awake. This was worse than school had ever been. I kept dozing off. Then my head would jerk, and I'd wake up again. One time I felt Christa jab me in the ribs. "Try not to snore," she whispered. Terrific! I could get in trouble even in my sleep.

I thought the class would never end. Maybe college wasn't as great as I'd thought. I sure wouldn't want to sit through many classes like this.

We met Xandy crossing the green on the way to Christa's next class. "So how do you like college life?" he asked.

"It's pretty boring."

"If you think that was boring," Christa said, "wait

till you get a load of my next class—economics. Even *I* fall asleep in that one."

"Look, she doesn't have to sit through that," Xandy said. "Why don't you hang out with me, Natalie? I don't have a class this next hour."

"Sure," I said.

"I'll take you up to my room," Xandy said. "Christa can meet us there after class."

Xandy's room was in the East Tower on a men's floor. It was a lot smaller than Christa's because it was a single. He had all sorts of neat stuff for juggling—colored balls, rings, pins, and even torches. He had a picture of himself and another kid juggling with real flames.

"That's my partner," he said. "We used to do shows together in high school."

"Don't you get burned when you juggle torches?" I asked.

Xandy grinned "Only if you catch the wrong end. Then you let go of it pretty fast."

"Can you show me how you do it?"

"Not on campus. Last time I tried it in the parking lot, somebody called the Campus Security." He started juggling with three red beanbags. "Watch. I'll give you a juggling lesson with these. You start with two of them. Like this."

He tossed both bags in the air and caught them in the opposite hands.

"That looks easy," I said. "Let me try." When I tossed the beanbags, they both landed on the floor.

Xandy picked them up. "There's a trick to it. You wait until the first bag is in the middle, just above your eye level. Then you toss the second bag. If you throw them at the same time, there's no way you can catch them."

I did it over and over, but no matter how hard I tried, I still dropped at least one of the bags every time.

"Here, watch me again." Xandy did a perfect double catch and handed the bags back to me. "Don't watch the beanbags. Keep your eyes right here." He held his finger just above my eye level. "I'll tell you when to toss the second bag. Okay . . . toss right."

I tossed.

"Now toss left."

I tossed the left bag, and I caught them both. "I did it. I really did it!"

Xandy patted me on the back. "Good start. Keep going with that for a while. I've got some reading to do for my next class. If you stand over there by the bed, you don't have to bend down so far to pick the beanbags up when you drop them."

I practiced for the next fifteen minutes. By then I could catch both bags every time.

Xandy got up from his desk. "You caught on pretty fast. Now for the big time. We'll add the third one."

"How can you catch three bags with two hands?"

"Simple," Xandy said. "You start with two bags in your right hand and one in the left. It's the same thing. Keep your eye on the spot above your head. Toss right, toss left, toss second right, catch left, catch right, catch second left."

I was really lost now. Beanbags were flying all over the place. Each time Xandy patiently explained it to me again. "Relax. You're tensing up and tossing the bags too far."

By the end of the hour I was able to do four catches before dropping a bag.

"You're picking this up much faster than your sister did," Xandy said. "You're really something."

What a day. So what if those stupid girls had laughed at me in the dining hall? They probably didn't even know how to juggle.

Chapter Fourteen

Things were quiet that night in the room. Christa hadn't finished her paper, and Beth was still working on her art project. They brought me back a pretty good meal—nothing hot, just what they could stuff in their pockets. I had two kinds of sandwiches, some fruit, and chocolate chip cookies. I stretched out on my sleeping bag, munching and watching TV.

I had decided to practice one more day before I amazed Christa with my juggling skills. That would give me something to do in the room when I was alone. Xandy promised not to tell Christa about my juggling lesson, so it would be a surprise.

Beth leaned back from her drawing board and stretched. "I can't believe how long this is taking. Maybe I should change my major."

Christa and I went over to look at her project. Beth had made some of the letters darker than others. She not only had the shape of the waves, but it was shaded so that it looked three-dimensional. "That's really beautiful," Christa said.

"Bet you couldn't do this on a computer, could you?" Beth asked. Christa shook her head. "No, probably not."

"So you finally admit it," Beth said. "Human talent wins out over the machine." She bent back over her drawing, smiling. "A couple more hours and this should be done. Maybe I'll even get some sleep tonight."

"I'm almost at the end, too," Christa said. "I should be ready to print this out in another hour. I hate these long projects."

"But just think how good we'll feel when we're finished," Beth said. "You'll turn your paper in tomorrow morning, and I'll take this to my four o'clock class. Tomorrow night, we can celebrate."

Christa undid her braid and ran her fingers through her hair. "You'd better believe it. We'll have a party, Natalie. Tomorrow's payday, so we can order pizza and stuff."

"You get paid to go to school?"

Beth laughed. "Not quite. We have campus jobs. I work three nights a week in the dining hall. Christa has it easy. She just shows movies to the cinema classes."

"It's not so easy when the projector breaks," Christa said, "which happens at least once a week. Anyway,

Nat, we'll finally have a chance to sit down and talk tomorrow night. The pressure will be off."

"Sounds great," I said. This was perfect. Right in the middle of the party, Xandy could announce that I had something special to show them. Then I'd stand up and juggle. I could hardly wait to see the expression on Christa's face. I felt under my pillow. There were the three beanbags that Xandy had let me borrow.

Tomorrow night I'd finally get a chance to talk to Christa, just like old times. I was really starting to feel at home here.

Christa dropped off my breakfast the next morning on her way to class. Beth skipped breakfast as usual. "Did you finish your projects last night?" I asked.

Christa picked up a bunch of papers fastened in a binder. "Here's mine. If I don't get an A on this, I give up."

"Mine's done, too," Beth said. "All I have to do is cut a mat for it, and I can do that right before calligraphy class. I have that hour free."

Christa grabbed her jacket. "Okay, Nat. I'm heading out for my eight o'clock, and I have one other class after that. You want to go with me or stay here?"

"Are they boring?" I asked.

Christa smiled. "The first one's okay, but the next one is deadly."

"I'll pass," I said.

As soon as Christa and Beth left the room, I started practicing. I was getting up to five catches now. Once it was even six. I couldn't wait to see Christa's face when I showed her what I had learned.

She almost caught me juggling when she came back after her classes. Luckily, I heard her talking to somebody in the hall. I just had time to stash the beanbags in my sleeping bag before she burst through the door.

"You're early," I said, trying to look innocent.

"You don't even have the music or TV on. What have you been doing to keep entertained?"

I shrugged. "I was watching something. I just turned it off."

Christa dug my lunch out of her pocket. "Here, enjoy. I have a free hour now, so we can go pick up my mail. There's usually a letter from Mom on Tuesdays."

"I know. She always writes to you on Sunday afternoon. I think she wrote to you right after she finished packing this week."

I ate my lunch as we walked across campus. Christa had to stop and get a book at the library, so I finished the last of my sandwich on the front steps. Then we went into the campus post office. There was a whole wall filled with mail boxes. Christa unlocked hers and opened it. "There it is, right on schedule," she said, pulling out a purple envelope. "I can spot Mom's letters a mile away. Come on, I'll get you a Coke."

We went downstairs to the snack bar. Christa bought pop for each of us and we took it over to a table by the window. The view from here was the same as the one from Christa's room—the lake stretching off into the distance—only today dark gray clouds were moving in. "Looks like it's going to rain," I said.

"Mmm," Christa said, not looking up from the letter. "It feels almost cold enough for snow."

"What does Mom say?" I asked, feeling just a slight twinge of homesickness.

Christa ran her fingers through her hair the same way Mom did. "It's mostly about Frank and how great he is. And about this wonderful trip that he surprised her with."

"Terrific," I said. "I can't get away from Frank even here. I don't suppose she mentions me, does she?"

Christa flipped through three pages. "I don't think so . . . oh, here you are. She says, 'Natalie sends her love.' "

"That's it?" I asked.

Christa nodded. "I'm afraid so." She finished reading the letter while I sipped my Coke and watched the clouds slide in over the lake.

Christa finally folded the letter and put it into her purse. "How have things been with Frank? He's not so bad, is he?"

"It's not just him, Christa. It's his mother. Mrs. Willderby wants to make us into clones of herself. She doesn't like anything about us. She doesn't like the way we dress. She doesn't like our house. She doesn't like the way Mom cooks."

"Well, Mom didn't marry Mrs. Willderby," Christa said.

"Frank treats me like a little kid," I said. "He doesn't even want me to be left alone for two seconds."

Christa raised her eyebrows. "You mean he's afraid you might do something stupid like run away?"

"I had to get out of there for a little while, Christa. With Carla gone, I'm so lonely."

"How old was I when Alyssa Rubino moved away?" Christa asked. "Must have been fifth or sixth grade, right?"

I shrugged. "I don't remember anybody named Alyssa Rubino."

"Oh, that's right. You were just a toddler then. Anyway, she was my only friend in the world. I was devastated when she left, but Mom said I'd make new friends."

"Sounds familiar," I said.

"Nat, she was right. By freshman year in high school, I had so many friends I was voted class president."

I slid down in my chair. "Freshman year in high school is a hundred years away."

Christa put her arm around me. "What I mean is, I

didn't make those friends all at once. It happened over the years. Then, when we moved and I had to start all over my junior year, it wasn't quite so scary. Just don't panic."

Christa made it sound so easy, but it seemed as if she'd always had lots of friends. It was hard to picture her being lonesome.

I finished my Coke, and we walked back toward the dorm. The sun broke through a hole in the clouds, making the leaves blaze bright with fall colors. We took a road that went along the edge of the campus.

Christa grabbed my hand and squeezed it as we walked. "It's kind of fun having you here, Nat. I think I've been more homesick than I realized." She pointed to a red brick building down the hill. "See that school over there? That's where Beth starts practice teaching next semester. Can you picture her standing up in front of a class of sixth graders?"

"Sixth graders?" I asked. "You mean it's a regular school like mine?"

Christa laughed. "Sure. What did you think they did, bring in fake students to practice on?"

It was only a short distance to the dorm. Christa gave me the key and went on to class. Instead of going in, I retraced my steps to look at the school. Some kids were just starting to come out of the front door—kids my age.

Suddenly I had a great idea. What if I could stay in

the dorm with Christa and Beth and go to that school? Mom and Frank could pay for my room and meals, just the way they did with Christa. Christa said she liked having me here, which is more than Frank had ever mentioned. Even Mom didn't seem to care whether I was home or not. All she cared about these days was cooking great meals and making the house organized for Frank. She'd never done that for Christa and me.

I'd tell Christa about my idea tonight at the party, right after my juggling act. I went back to the room and took out the beanbags. Xandy had said Christa could do about ten catches without stopping. The most I'd ever done was six. Maybe I could get up to ten by tonight.

I started juggling. At first I was too tense, and the beanbags kept getting away from me. I was tossing them too far. I took a deep breath and tried to relax. I worked my way up to four, then six. I looked at the clock. Christa should be coming back any minute. I had to keep practicing.

Six . . . seven . . . eight! That's when it happened. One of the beanbags flew across the room and landed on Beth's drawing board. An open bottle of ink tipped over, and before I could get to it, a black puddle spread over Beth's wave. Beth's beautiful wave!

I grabbed a towel and started blotting up the mess, but that spread the ink even more, covering the delicate lettering. I ran to the bathroom and wet the towel, squeezing most of the water out. Maybe I could wash the ink off the page. I started rubbing at the worst part of the ink blot, and before I realized it, the top layer of paper was peeling off in little shreds. I was making it worse instead of better.

Suddenly the door opened and Beth came in, carrying a big piece of poster board. She was smiling at first, but her face changed when she saw her wrecked project. "Natalie! What have you done?" She snatched the towel from my hands. "It's ruined. A whole week's work destroyed."

"I'm sorry," I mumbled.

"Sorry! You think that's going to make any difference to my calligraphy instructor? You think he's still going to give me a good grade if I just describe to him what's under this mess?" Beth burst into tears. "I needed an A in this course to bring up my average. Now I could lose my scholarship, and it's all your fault."

"What's going on? I could hear the shouting from the elevator." Christa stopped dead when she saw the drawing board. "Oh, Beth! What happened?"

"It's your sister." Beth spat out the words. "She knocked over the ink on my drawing board."

Christa turned on me. "Natalie, how could you be so clumsy? You should never have come to Corinthia in the first place. Little kids don't belong at college."

I ran out of the room and jumped on the elevator just before the doors closed. I could hear Christa yelling at me as she came down the hall, but she was too late. I ran out of the dorm, not even knowing where I was going.

The sun had slipped behind the hill, and it was starting to get cold. I'd go back into town and take the next bus home. It wouldn't kill me to spend a few days by myself. I was halfway across campus before I remembered that my bus ticket was in my suitcase in Christa's room. I couldn't face Christa and Beth again. I sat down on a bench by the fountains and tried to keep from crying. So much for the big celebration party. So much for making Christa proud of me when I showed her how I had learned to juggle. Christa and Beth would never let me stay here now. I didn't even want to stay.

I sat there for a long time watching the fountains. Pretty soon the lights went on—colored lights that made the fountains change from pink to blue to green. It was beautiful, but even that didn't cheer me up.

I pulled the sleeves of my sweatshirt over my hands, but the chill was creeping right into my bones and I couldn't stop shivering. I didn't know where I belonged anymore. That wasn't quite right. I knew exactly where I belonged—nowhere!

Chapter Fifteen

I stared at the fountains for a long time, so long that my eyes started doing strange things. Three spots of light were bouncing around from the other side of the water. At first I thought they were fireflies, but they were much too big and didn't blink on and off. I watched, fascinated, as they grew larger. Then I realized they were moving toward me, around the side of the fountain. Maybe I was about to be carried off to outer space by three strange light-creatures. I didn't even care. Whatever they did to me, it couldn't be any worse than what was happening to me on Earth.

Suddenly I could make out the shape of a person. It was Xandy, juggling balls of light. He tossed one to me. "Neat, huh? They glow in the dark. Want to try them out?"

"No thanks," I said, handing it back to him. "My juggling days are over."

Xandy sat down next to me on the bench. "I figured

that's what happened. You were practicing when you knocked over the ink?"

I nodded. "Christa's so mad, she's ready to kill me."

"Yeah, but she's worried, too." He took off his jacket and put it around my shoulders. "We've been searching all over for you. It's so cold, we all figured you'd be hiding inside somewhere."

I couldn't hold back the tears any longer. "I can't face them. I feel terrible about Beth's project."

I could barely see Xandy's face in the greenish glow. Three pinpoints of light reflected in each lens of his glasses. "Accidents happen," he said. "Besides, it might not be a total loss. Beth took the project over to her instructor to explain what happened. He might give her a break. Come on, let's go find your sister."

We didn't have to look for Christa. She came running to meet us on the walk outside the student union. "Natalie, I've been frantic. Where were you?"

"I'm sorry about everything that happened," I said. "I'm just a terrible person. I can't do anything right. That's why nobody wants me around."

Christa put her arm around me. "This whole mess has been partly my fault. I haven't given you enough attention. You probably got into trouble out of sheer boredom." She kept her arm around me as we walked back to the dorm.

"What are you going to do to me?" I asked.

"Boil you in oil," Xandy said in a Dracula voice.

"Then hang you out the window for the pigeons to eat. Heh-heh-heh."

"This is no time for jokes," Christa said, steering me into the elevator.

Xandy pushed the button for his floor. "Sorry. I can feel a real serious sister-to-sister-type discussion coming on. This is where I get off."

There were some other kids on the elevator, so Christa didn't say anything until we got back to her room. "I know you didn't do this on purpose, Natalie, but you can't stay here."

"What do you mean? I don't have anyplace to go. Besides, the week is already half over."

"It's only Tuesday," Christa said. "There's no telling what could happen between now and Sunday. I can't be responsible for you. I'm going to call Mom."

I climbed up on the top bunk and huddled by the wall, as if getting out of Christa's reach would stop her from calling. "I'll be good, Christa. I'll stay in the room the whole time. I'll just watch TV or something. You'll hardly know I'm here."

"You'd be bored silly," Christa said, digging a quarter out of her purse.

"But Christa, you promised you wouldn't tell Mom and Frank."

"That was only if everything went without a hitch."

"This is going to ruin their vacation," I said. "It's really their honeymoon, you know."

Christa came over to the edge of the bunk and looked up at me, her face serious. "Look, if you're miserable enough to run away from home, they'd better cut their honeymoon short and come home to work things out."

"They're going to kill me," I moaned, pulling Christa's comforter over my head.

"Possibly," Christa said, "but if you stay here and keep getting into trouble, *I'm* going to kill you, so you lose either way. Do you have the number where Frank and Mom can be reached?"

If Christa couldn't call Mom, I was safe until the end of the week. I kept my head covered, because Christa could always tell when I was lying just by looking at my eyes. "No," I said. "I'm not even sure where they are."

"Come on, Nat. Mom wouldn't go away without leaving you an emergency number. Wait a minute. I think she gave it to me in her letter." I peeked out from under the comforter and watched her dig through her purse and pull out Mom's purple envelope. "Here it is. She wanted me to know how to reach her in case something came up." Christa caught me peeking at her. "Something certainly did come up!"

I pulled down the comforter. "Okay, so you have to call Mom and Frank. Does that mean the party tonight is off?"

"The party," Christa said, "is definitely off." She

took the letter out to the phone in the hall. I could hear her dialing. "Yes, operator, this is a collect call from Christa." There was a long pause. "Mom? Oh, I'm so glad you're there. . . . No, nobody's sick or anything. . . . No, nobody's been in an accident. Mom, stop asking questions and listen! The problem is Natalie."

Chapter Sixteen

Mom and Frank told Christa they'd fly to Rochester the next morning, then pick up their car at the airport and drive up to Corinthia. I stood by Christa's window all morning, watching for Frank's tan Volvo station wagon on the lake road. I had barely slept all night. Beth had told me not to worry, that her professor was grading her on what was left of the project, but it didn't make me feel any better. From all the tossing and turning going on in Beth's and Christa's bunks, I don't think they slept very well, either. I could hardly wait to get out of there, but I wasn't looking forward to what I had to face at home.

Christa stopped back at the room between classes. "I picked up some lunch for you. No sign of Mom and Frank yet?"

"Not yet."

She dumped one set of books on her desk and picked up another. "Watching out the window won't make them come any faster."

"I'm not trying to make them come faster," I said. "Seeing Mom and Frank is about the last thing I want to do."

"I'm sorry I yelled at you, Nat." Christa gave me a hug. "I'm going to be in class until three, so I probably won't see you again before you leave. I hope you get things straightened out with Mom and Frank. Don't be afraid to tell them how you feel."

"I won't." Then I went back to the window after Christa left. Suddenly there was a knock at the door. My heart jumped into my throat. I must have missed seeing Frank's car while I was talking to Christa.

I opened the door, but it wasn't Mom and Frank. It was Xandy. "I was hoping I'd get a chance to say good-bye. Christa said your Mom is coming to pick you up."

"Yeah," I said. "Any minute now."

"Listen, I'm sorry my juggling lessons got you into trouble."

"It wasn't your fault. That reminds me . . ." I dug the juggling beanbags out from under my pillow. "I almost forgot to give these back to you."

Xandy pushed them back into my hands. "No, you keep them and practice at home. Then next time you come to visit, I'll teach you some harder moves."

"Christa and Beth will never let me come back. Even if they do, they won't let me juggle in the room."

"Sure they will. I'll talk them into it," Xandy said, messing up my hair. "After all, you're my best juggling student."

"Really? Do you think you could teach me how to juggle flaming torches?"

Xandy grinned. "Why not? We'll start with flaming chicken wings and work up. Just don't try it at home, okay?"

"I won't."

"See you, kid." Xandy winked at me and closed the door.

I went back to the window, and pretty soon I spotted a tan Volvo coming into town. It disappeared behind buildings for three or four minutes, then showed up on the road to the dorm. There were two people in the front seat. It had to be Mom and Frank. I picked up my suitcase and stood facing the door.

It seemed forever before somebody knocked. When I opened the door, Mom was there alone. She looked so mad, I started to cry before she said anything. Then she hugged me. "Natalie, why did you do this?"

"Dad was called away on business," I said.

"You found this out after we left?"

"No, I knew before, but I didn't want to go to Grandma's, so I thought of coming to Corinthia."

"Why did you have to lie? Why didn't you tell me what you wanted to do?"

"If I'd told you I wanted to take a bus alone to Corinthia, would you have let me?"

Mom cleared off a spot on Beth's bed and motioned for me to sit next to her. "I would have considered it. We could have talked it over."

"Frank wouldn't let me go off on my own in a million years, and you know it."

"Natalie, you're *my* daughter, not Frank's. I'm the one who decides what you're allowed to do."

"No, you're not, Mom. You let Frank and his mother run our lives. You've turned into a real wimp."

Mom got up and turned to face me. "I'm just trying to make us into a family."

"Well, I hate to break this to you, Mom, but it's not working."

"This isn't getting us anywhere," Mom said. "Come on. Frank's waiting in the car."

The trip home was the longest one of my life. Frank didn't seem to know what to say to me, which made for a lot of awkward silences. The worst thing was the look of disappointment on Mom's face. I would have felt better if she'd yelled at me for a while to get it out of her system. Now her anger hung over me like a cloud as I huddled miserably in the back seat.

Mom was going to blame me for everything. Maybe I was being spoiled and selfish. Maybe things couldn't be the way they were before, and I'd just have to get used to a new life. There was only one good thing about having to go home. Now I'd be there for Carla's phone call Friday night.

We finally pulled into the driveway. I followed Mom and Frank up the front walk. Mom unlocked the door and went in. Suddenly she stopped and turned back.

"We're in the wrong house," she said. "How could we have . . . ?" She turned again. "No, this is our house. What's happened to it?"

I looked around the living room. All of our furniture was gone. In its place were a white modern couch that wrapped around three sides of the room, a white rug, a chrome-and-glass coffee table, and some weird modern lamps. The whole room was white, silver, and glass. Even the walls were painted white.

"I don't believe this," Frank said. "Mother must have started in on this the second we left home. I gave her an extra set of keys in case there was an emergency."

"When she said she'd take care of everything," Mom gasped, "I never dreamed she'd just go ahead and have it done. I thought she was going to come back with samples—things to choose from."

"So did I," Frank said. "Do you . . . like the new look?"

Mom ran her fingers over the arm of the couch. "I . . . well, it's different, but it's . . . elegant. Your mother has good taste, Frank."

Frank looked around the room. "Oh yes. She does have that."

Mom turned to me. She had that bright phony smile on again. "Doesn't the room look beautiful, Natalie?"

"No, Mom," I said. "It looks like the inside of a refrigerator. I hate it."

Just then Mrs. Willderby came down the stairs. "Good heavens. What are you doing home so soon? I was upstairs dialing 911, thinking you were burglars. But then I heard your voices."

"We had an unexpected change of plans," Mom said, giving me a pointed look.

Mrs. Willderby stopped at the bottom of the stairs and gave her magic wand gesture. "Ta-dah! What do you think of the transformation? I was just looking at the master bedroom. That's my next project."

"I don't intend to do any entertaining in the bedroom," Mom said. "I want it left the way it is."

"Nonsense," Mrs. Willderby said. "That room could use some sprucing up. But you haven't said what you think of the living room." She smiled expectantly.

"Natalie's right," Mom said. "This room looks exactly like the inside of a refrigerator—cold and unlivable. I know you meant well, Mother Willderby, but this is our home. I never would have chosen these things."

Mrs. Willderby's "wattles" quivered. "I'll have you know Danielle DeVeaux is the finest decorator in the city. She has exquisite taste."

"Well, Danielle DeVeaux doesn't live here." Mom stood up and stormed across the thick rug, leaving indentations where she had stepped. "This isn't a room you can live in. This is a room for entertaining important people. And you know something, Mother Willderby? The important people in my life are my family—my children and my husband. This isn't a room for a family. This is a room for visiting dignitaries."

Mrs. Willderby turned to Frank. "Are you going to let your wife talk to me like that?"

"Anne's right, Mother. You're way out of line here. You should have consulted us before going ahead."

"Well, I never . . ." Mrs. Willderby pulled her coat out of the closet. "I'll have these things returned to the store. They're obviously much too good for you." She pushed past Frank. "I feel sorry for you, Frank. Your wife is a common woman."

"I feel sorry for me, too," Frank said. "My mother is an insufferable snob." He had to step out of the way as the door slammed.

The three of us just stood there looking at each other for a few seconds, then Frank started to laugh. "Anne, I don't think anyone has told Mother off in her whole lifetime. You certainly made up for that tonight."

"I'm sorry, Frank. She made me so mad I lost control. I've kept my feelings inside for too long."

"Don't be sorry," Frank said. "You only did what I should have done a long time ago. It always seemed easier to let Mother have her own way, but she has a habit of taking over if you let her. From now on we'll make decisions as a family. Mother will just have to accept us as we are—all of us."

"You and I are so different from each other, Frank,"

Mom said. "If I really start saying what I think instead of trying to please you all the time, I'm afraid we'll never agree on anything. Natalie has some pretty strong ideas of her own, and she needs to be heard, too."

"Look," Frank said, "this is going to take some getting used to. I was trying to enforce Mother's rules, but they don't apply to us. There's no reason why we can't all say what we think and make compromises. Meanwhile, I'm starved. Anybody want to order out for pizza?"

"I'd rather have chicken wings," I said.

"To tell the truth," Mom said, "I'd rather have a meatball sub."

Frank smiled and dialed the phone. "Is this Eatsa Pizza? I'd like to order a small pepperoni pizza, an order of chicken wings, and a meatball sub."

Mom tapped him on the shoulder. "With extra onions and hot peppers."

Frank cringed. "With extra onions and hot peppers."

After dinner, I went out to sit on the back steps and think things over. That's when I noticed a note hanging on the garage door. It read: "Salvation Army: The furniture to be picked up is in garage. Door not locked."

I opened the door and went inside. There was all of

our old stuff shoved into a pile in the middle of the garage. I curled up in the corner of the couch, expecting to feel comforted by its familiar shape. I ran my hand over the seat of the couch and felt the lump where a broken spring was pushing through. In the late afternoon sun coming through the window, I could see all of the stains and faded places on the upholstery and the chips and scratches in the wood.

It's funny how you always remember things as being perfect. Life seemed great when it was just Christa, Mom, and me, and it was even better before that when Dad lived with us. But if it was so great, why did Mom and Dad get a divorce? I kept wanting to make things go back to the way they were. Maybe change wasn't so bad, as long as I had some say in the decisions. Besides, I could think of worse people to have for a stepfather than Frank.

"There you are. We wondered where you went." Mom ducked under the garage door and came in, still squinting from the sunlight. "Our furniture! So this is what Frank's mother did with it." She squeezed into the seat next to me. A bookcase was taking up most of the couch, so there was barely room for the two of us. "Well," Mom said, looking around. "This feels more like home, doesn't it?"

"I guess so," I said.

"Can you believe the nerve of that old crow, calling me a common woman?"

"Hen," I said.

"What?"

"Mrs. Willderby doesn't look like a crow. She looks like a hen."

Mom laughed. "Of course—Attilla the Hen! You're very observant, Natalie." She put her arm around me and I rested my head against her shoulder.

"I feel awful about bringing you back from your honeymoon early, Mom."

"Actually, neither of us was sorry to come back," Mom said. "We had rain the whole time, and it was predicted to last the rest of the week, so we never got to the beach." She lifted my chin so she could see my face. "What upsets me is your running away. I keep thinking of all the things that might have happened to you on the way to Christa's."

"Nothing happened. I was fine."

"I know, but don't ever do that again. Come to me and talk things over when you're upset."

"Will you really listen from now on?" I asked. "You didn't before."

Mom leaned her head back on the couch and closed her eyes. "I know. I was too busy trying to be a new bride, trying to please Frank, trying to make myself into somebody I'm not. I wasn't thinking about what all this was doing to you—or me—and I'm sorry." She opened her eyes and looked at me. "Let's try to be a family now—the three of us, and Christa, too, when she's home."

"Sure, Mom," I said. "But promise me one thing."

"What's that?"

"I don't want Frank to adopt me."

"We've never even considered it, Nat. In the first place, I doubt that your father would agree to it."

"Well, it's a good thing because I'd hate to spend the rest of my life with a name like Natalie Willderby."

"I never thought of that," Mom said. "It sounds like a nursery rhyme character." She leaned back and laughed, then jumped up suddenly. "Ouch! I forgot about this broken spring." She looked around at the pile of junk in the garage. "Maybe we do need some new furniture. What do you think?"

"Not that stuff that Mrs. Willderby got," I said.

"No, that's going back to the store, and we can move our old things back in for now. But when Christa comes home for Thanksgiving, we'll all go furniture shopping together. I'm sure we'll find something we all like."

"Without Danielle DeVeaux?" I asked.

Mom smiled. "Yes, definitely without Danielle De-Veaux."

Chapter Seventeen

I didn't feel like going to school the next day, but I couldn't think of an excuse. Even though things seemed a little better at home, nothing would be changed at school. It would be me against the world, with no Carla to make it bearable.

As if things weren't bad enough, we had a sub. Her name was Miss Blandly, and she usually subbed at the primary school. "Now, boys and girls, let's go around the room and tell about what we did over our mini-vacation."

"Let's not," someone said from the back of the room.

Miss Blandly pretended she didn't hear and started calling out names from her seating chart. Most of the kids said they had just hung out at home. Anthony Argento said he slept the whole two days, nonstop.

Berna Jean Farber and the Innies had gone to the mall to pick out new outfits. Big surprise!

All of a sudden it was my turn. "Natalie Hanson?"

Miss Blandly said my name like a question. "Would you like to share with us?" Why did primary teachers always talk about sharing?

"I went to college," I said, ignoring the muffled snorts from the Innies. "I went to visit my sister at Corinthia College. I stayed in the dorm and everything. I even got to watch when she did the weather forecast for her TV class and . . ." I looked around the room. Everybody was watching me. I had to say something else. "And I learned how to juggle."

Miss Blandly's eyebrows shot up. "Really! How interesting. Would you care to give a demonstration?"

"I'd love to," I said, "but I didn't bring my juggling beanbags."

"Never fear," said Miss Blandly in her sing-songy voice. "I just happen to have some in my briefcase. Substitute teachers must be prepared for anything, you know."

The odds of getting a substitute teacher with juggling beanbags had to be about a million to one, right? Maybe even a zillion. I never would have mentioned juggling if I thought I'd actually have to do it. The Innies were shooting looks back and forth to each other like Ping-Pong balls.

I walked slowly to Miss Blandly's desk, hoping a major earthquake might hit before I got there. After all, we'd never had an earthquake before. We were certainly due for one.

She handed me the beanbags, and I took a deep

breath. Then I started. "One . . . two . . . three . . ."
I dropped one and started over. "Not warmed up," I
mumbled.

I pictured Xandy in my mind, and I pretended I was
him. I was getting into the rhythm of it now, and some
of the kids joined in the counting.

". . . four . . . five . . . oops! six . . ." I got over-
confident for a minute, carried away. There . . . back
in the groove.

". . . eight . . . nine . . . ten . . ." They were starting to clap in rhythm to the catches, and they carried
me all the way up to fifteen, when I dropped one on
Berna Jean's desk.

"Natalie," Miss Blandly said. "That's amazing. You
certainly put your vacation to good use."

I was a hard act to follow. Everybody else was pretty
boring. Then we went on to the usual stuff like math
and reading. On the way to lunch, Berna Jean tapped
me on the arm. "That must have been so exciting,
going to college," she said. "What do the college girls
wear?"

I shrugged. "Well, they don't wear the stuff you see
in the magazines. They dress pretty much like I do.
Lots of people thought I was a college student when I
was there."

Berna Jean's eyes grew wide as she looked over
my outfit—early Salvation Army with accessories
from Volunteers of America. "That's fascinating.

Why don't you sit with us at lunch and tell us more?"

I followed the Innies into the cafeteria and over to their usual table. Adrian Brower came in a few minutes later with a girl I didn't know. Adrian's class was way down at the other end of the school, so it took her longer to get there. They started to sit down, but Berna Jean waved the new girl away. "Our table's full."

"We have plenty of seats," Adrian said. "This is Jessie Beck. She's from my class."

"You know the rules," Berna Jean said. "At least three of us have to agree on somebody before they can sit at our table."

"Well, it's a stupid rule," Adrian said, getting up. "It's a free country. People can sit where they want to. I wouldn't sit here if you paid me a hundred dollars."

Berna Jean's eyes narrowed as she watched Adrian walk away. "I don't like her attitude lately. She's changed."

"She sure has," Kimberly said. "She'd better watch out."

"Never mind Adrian for now." Berna Jean turned to me and smiled. "Now, Natalie. Tell us what the college girls are really wearing."

I spent the rest of the lunch period giving the Innies a fashion lesson. By the time the bell rang, they could hardly wait to start dressing like bag ladies. The trouble was, on them it would probably look good. I was picturing them on the way home. I guess that's why I didn't hear the footsteps following me.

"Natalie?" a voice said as I started up my sidewalk. I turned around. It was Adrian Brower. "Some of the kids at lunch said you went to visit your sister at college this week. I'd like to hear what it was like."

I was ready to launch into another fashion lecture. "Well, most of the girls are wearing . . ."

"No," she interrupted. "I don't care about the clothes. I just wondered what the dorms and classes are like. My sister went away to school this year, too, but she's way out in Michigan." She took out her wallet and showed me a picture. "This is her—Angela. I really miss her. I have a couple of brothers still at home, but . . . it's not the same, you know?"

"Yeah," I said. "It was really nice to see Christa. Sometimes you don't appreciate sisters until they move away."

"You want to come over to my house for a while?" Adrian asked. "I live about a block away, on Orchard."

"Sure. Come in for a second while I drop off my stuff." I dumped my books and jacket on the couch, then thought about Frank. "Just a minute. I have to leave a note." I hung my jacket in the hall and put my books on the corner of the desk. I was halfway through writing the note when the phone rang.

It was Berna Jean. "Hi, Natalie. Mom is taking me and my friends shopping. Want to come along?"

"You're going right now?" I said. I looked over at Adrian. She was standing by the door, twisting a hunk of hair around her finger. I was being invited instead of her. If I turned Berna Jean down, it might be the last time I ever got asked. You just didn't say no to the Innies.

"Well?" Berna Jean's voice was getting impatient. "Are you coming along or not? We could pick you up in a few minutes."

"I don't know. This is kind of short notice."

Adrian put her hand on the doorknob. "If you want to do something else, it's fine. We can talk some other time."

"No, wait!" I said.

"We can't wait," Berna Jean said. "My mom's already got the car running in the driveway."

"I'm really busy right now, Berna Jean," I said. "Maybe some other time."

There was a brief silence at her end of the line. "Fine," Berna Jean said, and the receiver clicked in my ear.

"Same to you," I said to the dial tone.

Adrian smiled. "Not many people have the guts to say no to Berna Jean."

For the rest of the week the Innies were nastier to me than ever. It didn't matter as much, though. I looked forward to lunch every day because I could eat with Adrian and some of her friends. For an Innie,

Adrian turned out to be pretty nice. I met some other kids, too. They had heard about my juggling and wanted me to give them lessons. It wasn't the same as having a best friend like Carla, but at least I wasn't lonesome anymore. I'd have lots of news to tell Carla when she called.

Friday night at eleven I was standing by the phone in the kitchen. Mom and Frank had already gone to bed, and the house was so quiet I could hear the clock on the stove ticking. I was thinking about all of the things I wanted to tell Carla. It would be hard to fit everything into twenty minutes.

When it got to be eleven-fifteen, I poured myself a glass of milk and sat down at the kitchen table. What was keeping Carla? She couldn't forget, could she?

Another ten minutes went by. Suddenly I realized what had happened. Cleveland was probably in a different time zone from Rochester. That meant that eleven o'clock in Cleveland was really midnight here. I ran into the living room and looked up the time zone map in my social studies book. I searched through the central time zone for Cleveland. Finally I found it—in the eastern time zone, the same as Rochester.

I got a sick feeling in the pit of my stomach. Carla had forgotten about our phone schedule. Even worse, maybe she'd decided to give up on our friendship, the way she had with all of the others. If my letter never reached her, or if she got it but didn't write back, I'd never be able to find her. Maybe Carla had the right idea. Why bother to make friends, anyway? You only end up getting hurt.

I went back into the kitchen to turn out the light. Just as I hit the switch, the phone rang. I tipped over a chair, trying to get to it in the dark.

"Carla?"

"Who else would be calling this late?" she said. "I fell asleep watching TV. Next time it's my turn, I'll set the alarm."

"I'm so glad you called," I said. "Wait till you hear what I have to tell you."

We both talked as fast as we could, trying to get all our news in. "I just had the greatest idea, Carla."

"Make it quick, Nat. Our twenty minutes is almost up."

"Listen," I said. "I think we should both go to Corinthia when we get out of high school. Maybe we could be TV/radio majors like Christa, and we could room together."

Carla thought for a minute. "Okay. But that's a long time from now."

"Not really," I said. "Only seven years."